Operation Exodus

by

Gene Masters

Published in the United States of America by
Escarpment Press, Indian Land, SC

www.escarpmentpress.weebly.com
Hendersonville, NC

For Tom Burke, in memoriam

Prologue

Kandahar Province, Afghanistan

The SEALs, the Congressman, and the three USAID workers were pinned down in an isolated building in the middle of nowhere. SEAL platoon Two-Four numbered eighteen men, but this mission was supposed to be kept low-key, so as not to call attention to the presence of Congressman Longstreet. Besides, it was a simple "in-and-out" (no Taliban were supposed to be anywhere near this area), so Jake had left a half-dozen of his men back at base. Now he wished he hadn't; he could have used those six additional riflemen about now.

"Conciliation Base, this is Two-Four Leader, over."

"Conciliation Base here, go ahead Two-Four Leader."

"We have a situation here, Base. Taliban have location surrounded. Have six friendly natives down, presumed dead, one SEAL wounded, needs medevac. Four civilians and eleven SEALs okay for now. Could use some help, over."

"Roger that, Two-Four. Gunship or jets? Over."

"Gunship, Base. Over."

"Gunship and one medevac, aye, Two-Four. Need coordinate readout. Over."

Jake Lawlor looked at the numbers on his satellite radiotelephone, and read them off: "Two-Four is at coordinates 31.523-330, 66.190-648. Over."

"Conciliation Base has your posit 31.523-330, 66.190-648, verify, over."

"Two-Four verifies."

"Roger that. Uh, Base requests status of Rebel, over"

Should have known that was coming, Jake thought. "Rebel" was the code name for Congressman Longstreet.

"Rebel is okay."

"Roger that, Rebel okay, will get gunship and medevac on the way. Conciliation Base, out."

* * * * *

Jacob Joseph Lawlor Jr. was third-generation Navy, and his father and grandfather — both submariners — had achieved flag rank. But Jake had eschewed submarines and, instead, had opted to become a SEAL. Now, it occurred to him, fleetingly, that perhaps that may have been an unwise decision.

Even before the shooting started, Jake had evaluated the tactical situation: The building, situated on flat ground and in a relatively open area, was made of fitted stone, no mortar, about ten meters wide and four meters deep. The back, north wall was solid, no windows. Only opening in the front, south wall was a low doorway. Windows at both ends. Turf roof.

The congressman and the USAID workers were huddled together in the back of the hut, against the north wall. The SEALs had set up the wooden table in front of them, between them and the entrance. It didn't provide much protection, but that's all there was.

Jake realized that the safety provided by the solid stone back wall cut both ways. Sure, Taliban bullets couldn't penetrate the wall, and even a rocket propelled grenade — an RPG — couldn't go through it. But it gave the Taliban fighters excellent cover for approaching the building from the rear. There was nothing to prevent them from sneaking around from the back and then suddenly appearing at either of the windows, or at the doorway, and firing into the hut. With that in mind, Jake had stationed three of his men in strategic positions inside the hut, each one assigned to cover an access port.

Of course, there's nothing to stop the Tallies from firing an RPG from a safe distance through any access port and wiping out everyone inside, Jake thought. *Nor could we stop them from putting a mortar round through the roof and accomplishing the same thing. And Tallies always have RPGs and mortars. So exactly why haven't they already wiped the place clean? Because they want live prisoners, that's why, or at least one live prisoner — they want Longstreet! Shit! Nobody was supposed to know he was even in country! So much for security! One of the Afghan "friendlies" at the base must have sold him out. Nothing to do now but sit it out and see what develops.*

Just for a second, Jake's thoughts drifted off to a black cat named Moses, and the cat sitter, a dark-haired Italian-American beauty ironically named Julie O'Leary, back in East Beach. Then he wondered, *Why now? Of all times, why am I thinking about Julie when I need to pay attention to business . . .*

"The Tallies want to take the VIP alive," Chief Petty Officer William Cole, Jake's platoon chief, said aloud, waking him from his momentary reverie, and echoing his earlier thoughts. Cole had been the senior enlisted man in Jake's platoon from the beginning, and the two of them had become fast friends.

"Right," Jake agreed. "They could have wiped this place clean out long ago, with an RPG round or a mortar shell."

"Exactly," Cole said. "Don't think they'd much care if they killed *us*, or the USAID guys for that matter, so it has to be Longstreet they're after. Feather in their cap if they can pull off capturing a U.S. Congressman, and he's apparently no good to 'em dead."

Then there were explosions heard coming from outside the hut.

"That's coming from the road," Cole observed.

Jake approached the doorway cautiously. The doorway, like the windows, was covered by just a ragged curtain. Jake, keeping low, moved the curtain just enough to see out onto the roadway. He was greeted with a bullet, glancing off the side of the building, just to the right of his head—*but* he had had enough time to see what the explosions were about. The SEALs' two armored personnel carriers (APCs) and the USAID workers' Chevy Suburban were in flames.

"There went our rides, Billy," Jake said with obvious dismay.

"Well, now we know for sure they have RPGs if they want to use them," Cole replied.

"Roger that," Jake agreed. "It's Longstreet, all right. They could care less about the rest of us, but the Tallies definitely want Longstreet alive."

* * * * *

The Fourth Platoon, SEAL Team Two, was embedded with the Third Battalion, Second Marine Division at Conciliation Base, in Kandahar Province, Afghanistan. The SEALs were in the last month of a six-month tour. They were due for rotation back to the States in three weeks, give or take a day or two. The SEAL platoon leader, Navy Lieutenant Jacob Joseph Lawlor, Jr., had been quick to point out, to anyone interested, that thus far on this deployment, none of his men had suffered so much as a paper cut—not until today, anyway.

What a laugh. All the SEALs had to do was to quietly escort the USAID workers and their special guest to the meeting with some Afghan tribal chieftains, stand guard while they talked, and then escort them back to base. That was all. Nobody said anything about the meeting being broken up by the Taliban. To the contrary, Intel had said that nobody knew the congressman was in country, and, besides, all the Taliban in the area had skedaddled across the southern border into Pakistan. No Taliban, no sweat, right?

The day had dawned hot and bright, not a cloud in sight. Now, early in the afternoon, it was even hotter, the air heavy, with the desert glaring back at an unrelenting sun. The SEALs were in modified kit: desert fatigues, Kevlar helmets and flak jackets, standard M4 rifles (as distinct from the M4a1 rifles they carried on special ops), and no packs—*but* plenty of water. Failing to stay hydrated in this climate was not an option.

Jake's introduction to the congressman had been brief, but cordial. The Marine major escorting Longstreet had made the introduction: "Representative Robert Longstreet, this is Navy SEAL Lieutenant Jake Lawlor. Lt. Lawlor, Representative Longstreet. Congressman Longstreet represents Mississippi's Twenty-Sixth District, Lieutenant, and is the House Minority Whip."

"Pleased to meet you, Sir," Jake responded, wondering what it was, exactly, that a "House Minority Whip" did.

"And, I you, Jake. But please call me Bob!"

"Yes, Sir . . . err . . . Bob"

Representative Longstreet smiled broadly. "Your reputation precedes you, Lieutenant. Understand you're third generation Navy, and that the Lawlor name is the stuff of legend. The major, here, tells me you're more than living up to it."

"The major's too kind, Sir."

"Call me Bob."

"Yes, Sir . . . Bob."

"Wanted to join the Marines, myself," the congressman mused, "but they wouldn't have me because of a miserable heart murmur. Fortunately for me, that couldn't keep me from running for public office, instead—although some of my constituents might not agree!" He grinned at his little joke. "Sorry to complicate your mission," he continued, "but education is my job in the House, and I understand this little meeting with the Afghans is all about that—building schools for the children, and such—so I thought I'd tag along. Maybe learn a few things!" He flashed another smile.

Jake smiled back, deciding he liked the man.

* * * * *

The six tribesmen at the meeting had just gone outside the building to confer in private when the shooting started. Now, Jake's second in command, Lieutenant Junior Grade Henry "Hank" Greenburg, lay in quiet agony with a shattered femur. Hank had been hit when a stray AK-47 round came in through the front door. Special Warfare Operator First Class (SO1) Clarence "Slewfoot" Wilson (the closest thing the platoon had to a medic on this trip) had put a tourniquet on Hank's leg, and set it as best he could. A morphine shot dulled the pain somewhat, and a hastily-applied dressing at least hid the gaping wound and the exposed, splintered bone. But Hank had lost a lot of blood in the process. He needed that medevac.

"How you doing, Hank?" Jake asked.

"Lousy, Skipper, really, really lousy. I hurt like hell. I can hardly stand it. Honestly don't think I'm gonna make it."

"Bullshit, Hank. You're only at forty percent."

Despite the pain, Greenburg laughed. In BUDS (Basic Underwater Demolition/SEALs) training, all officers and enlisted candidates went through "hell week." Hell week consisted of five and a half days of continuous torture, featuring swimming, running, and rock portage in rubber raiding craft. The trainees endured cold, wet, and exhaustion—and did it all on four hours sleep, total. When they were thoroughly blitzed, and didn't think they had one iota more to give, that's when their observer/instructors would say: "You're only at forty percent." The implication was, of course, that if you would only dig down deep enough, you would find that other sixty percent, and be able to give that too.

"Screw you, Skipper." Greenburg said. "I'm at least at fifty."

* * * * *

"Mr. Greenburg needs that medevac bad, L-T," Chief Cole volunteered. L-T: The spoken letters that described his rank. That was pretty much how all the enlisted members of his platoon addressed Jake. It was a sobriquet that expressed at once both familiarity and respect.

"I know, Billy, I know," replied Jake. "Now all we have to do is convince those Tallies out there that they need to be so kind as to clear out and let the medevac chopper land."

Earlier, before the Taliban had wounded Greenburg and wasted the Afghans, the four tribal leaders had sat on cushions behind that selfsame, low table that now shielded the USAID workers. For the most part, the Afghans wore light, flowing robes of muted earth colors, their heads swathed in scarves. Their apparent leader, an ancient man with flowing white whiskers, was, unlike the others, dressed entirely in white. The

USAID workers were dressed like tourists: cargo shorts, tee shirts, and ball caps. Congressman Longstreet had worn sharply-creased khaki slacks and a white dress shirt with an open collar.

Two other tribesmen had stood guard inside the hut, while two others stood guard outside. The guards were the only ones armed (although the others carried ceremonial knives). Each guard carried, of course, the ubiquitous AK-47 rifle, also the weapon of choice for the Taliban, as well as most of the word's insurgent groups, and quite a few national armies as well.

The tribesmen and two of the USAID workers were speaking Pashto, a language Jake didn't understand, nor did the congressman, who just stood off in the background, the other USAID worker interpreting for him. He said nothing, as he intently observed the give-and-take between the USAID workers and the Afghans.

One of Jake's team, SO1 (Special Warfare Operator, First Class) Foster Fowles, spoke Pashto fluently, and was able to follow the negotiations. The tribal leaders were arguing with the USAID workers, and Jake could see by the frown on Fowles' face, that the discussion was not going well.

Jake sidled up to Fowles. "What's going on?" he asked.

"The old man, the guy in white, the 'Elder Dude,' is their boss, and, well, he's not thrilled that the USAID guys won't build his village a school unless he agrees to let girls attend," Fowles explained.

" 'Elder Dude' says Allah doesn't want his people to waste time educating girls," Fowles continued, "and the USAID guys are saying 'No girls, no school,' and neither side is willing to back down. The 'Younger Dude' was trying to get 'Elder Dude' to reconsider, and the 'Elder Dude' just gets more pissed."

"And the congressman's not saying anything."

"Not so far," Fowles agreed.

Then the tribesmen got up and made ready to leave. "What now? They done?" Jake asked Fowles.

"Not exactly," Fowles answered. " 'Elder Dude' says he and his people need to talk privately, so they're going outside to parley. He *says* they'll be back."

And no sooner had all six of the tribesmen cleared the front door, when the firing began. It all came down so fast that the two guards outside the door never got off a shot, and Hank Greenburg was rolling on the floor in pain, clutching his shattered leg. The two inside guards had run outside and started shooting, but they were dropped not far beyond the doorway. None of the Afghans made it back to the hut. When the occasional breeze parted the door curtain, Jake could see their fallen bodies scattered like so many dry leaves in the wind.

While Wilson attended to Greenburg, Jake and Cole herded the civilians to the back of the hut and set the table up in front of them.

"What's the prognosis, Jake?" Longstreet asked calmly, "We gonna be able to make it out of here?"

"We're sure as hell gonna try, Sir," Jake replied.

"Bob," Longstreet corrected, smiling. "Do what you need to do, lieutenant. And don't mind us. We'll just try and stay out of your way while you do your job." He looked at the three USAID guys and nodded. They nodded back, but Jake noted that they were nowhere near as composed as Longstreet.

"Will do, Bob," Jake said.

* * * * *

It wasn't long after the RPG rounds had destroyed their vehicles, and Jake was about to get on the horn to base to tell them that they now also needed a ride home, when the groaning was heard from outside the doorway.

"Somebody's alive out there," Cole said. "We goin' after them?" It was more of a statement than a question.

"That's what we do," Jake replied.

"I'll go, L-T," Cole said, his handsome black face lit with a grin.

"Not so fast, Billy. Somebody's got to stay and mind the store. I'll take three guys, and we'll drag back anyone who's alive out there. You and a fire team cover us."

"Why do you get to have all the fun? The brass *always* sends out the grunts to do the tough stuff!"

"Don't be such an asshole, Chief. Just make sure we don't get killed out there, okay?"

"Got your six, L-T, always, but no heroics."

"No heroics, Billy. So, before I go out there, I'm gonna call some artillery down on those Tallies' asses."

Jake got on the satellite radiotelephone. "Conciliation Base, this is Two-Four Leader. Over."

"This is Conciliation Base. Over."

"Base, SEAL Two-Four under fire, need some artillery. Over."

"Base has your posit 31.523-330, 66.190-648, verify. Over." Jake rechecked the numbers on his phone just to be sure.

"Two-Four verifies. Please stay at least a hundred meters from posit. Otherwise all about fair game. Over."

"Roger that, Two Four. First rounds overhead in about five minutes. Anything else? Over."

"Affirmative, Base. Taliban have destroyed our vehicles. Now need rides back to base. Also note that enemy force definitely equipped with Romeo Papa Golf. Over."

"Roger that, Two-Four. Definite Romeo Papa Golf. Have already dispatched Marine gunship and medevac. Will follow with transport. Understand you're busy, but keep Base advised. Over."

"Roger that, Conciliation Base, Two-Four Leader, out." Jake was turning to Cole as shots rang out from inside the building, coming from the west wall, M4 rounds aimed at the east window. Jake looked over in time to hear the grunt as a scarf-covered head in the east window turned to hamburger.

"Good shot, Janelli," Jake said.

"Okay, Billy, I'll take Smith and Claridge with me. Leave Janelli and Bonsignore covering the windows. You take the other guys, and cover us. Watch your flanks. The Tallies will surely try sneaking up the side of the building to get to us from behind. Maybe even go up on the roof. We go when the first shells land."

Jake frog-walked over to Longstreet and the USAID workers and told them what the SEALs were planning, and warned them to stay low and sit tight—and that things were about to get *very* loud. Longstreet listened calmly and carefully to the plan, and just nodded. Looking frightened, the USAID workers also said nothing, but they too nodded their understanding. Then Jake turned to Cole. "Set it up, Billy," he said. "We'll move when the first shell lands."

"Roger that, L-T." Cole sounded out the orders. "There appear to be some of the friendlies outside who are still alive, and the lieutenant is going out after them. Smith and Claridge,

11

you're with the lieutenant. Slew, Tansey, Fowles, Lindsey, and Chou, you're with me. We're covering the lieutenant and the others from outside the doorway. Janelli and Bonsignore, you still have window duty. Now when we move, gentlemen, be sure to stay the hell out of Janelli's and Bonsignore's lines of fire."

Just about then, the first of the artillery rounds landed. *BA-BOOM!* Cole grinned. "That's our cue, men. Lindsey and Chou, you'll watch our flanks. Tallies will try to come 'round the side of the building. Might even try scaling the roof. Now let's go."

To say the rescue operation went like clockwork would be a downright lie. Noise and confusion reigned. Jake and the two men with him crawled out the doorway, and drew immediate fire. If the artillery kept any Taliban heads down, and it must have, it was hard to tell from the overall amount of the initial incoming fire. It wasn't until the other SEALs fanned out behind them and returned the incoming fire, that the rounds aimed at Jake, Claridge, and Smith became less intensive.

There was noise everywhere, and from every direction. Shots were being fired from behind them and in front of them. There were the *brrrp! brrrp! brrrp!* of the M4s, and the ragged *brapt! brapt! brapt!* of the AK-47s. There were shots being fired inside the building as well: Janelli and Bonsignore firing at peeping Toms. And the artillery, shells exploding *BA-BOOM! BA-BOOM! BA-BOOM!* continually, incessantly, none thankfully nearby. It was bedlam.

Fortunately for the SEALs, and thanks to the artillery, the Taliban fighters were unable to stick their heads up long enough to aim and fire accurately. One SEAL, however, SO3 Jim Tansey, took a round full in the chest. His flak jacket stopped the round, but the impact knocked him off his feet. About twenty seconds later, cursing, clutching at his bruised chest, he regained his feet and emptied the rest of his clip in the direction of the offending round. "Easy, Tansey," Cole shouted above the din, "we don't have any ammo to waste."

Meanwhile, Jake and the two men with him were crawling on their bellies at double-time (if such was really possible) to get to the bodies of the tribesmen. Bullets fired by the SEALs behind them and the Taliban in front of them were whizzing close by all around them, and the artillery shells could be heard piercing the air high overhead and exploding everywhere. Occasionally, a bullet would kick up some soil ahead as well. Jake noticed that some of these were kicking the dirt *forward.* "Somebody's shooting at us from behind," he shouted above the din to Claridge and Smith. They turned to see that an intrepid Taliban had climbed up onto the roof and was shooting at them over the heads of Cole and the others. Smith aimed and fired, the M4 set on three-round burst mode, *brrrp! brrrp! brrrp!* and three 5.56 mm NATO rounds dropped the roof climber where he stood.

Back to crawling forward. The first two downed tribesman Jake and the others had encountered were the outside guards, and they were very dead. Smith and Claridge took their AK-47s, and crawled onward, right behind Jake. The cacophony continued around, above, and in front of them. They were surprised when the next body they reached, one of the younger tribesmen, the one Fowles had called "Younger Dude," spoke. He spoke Pashto, of course, so nobody there could understand him, but apparently, he had been playing possum, and was unhurt. Smith handed him the guard's rifle he had been carrying. The tribesman took it and began to fire back at the Taliban from the prone position. He was careful to fire only

13

when he had a target. Jake noted with satisfaction that when one of the Taliban exposed himself, the tribesman invariably dropped him with a well-aimed bullet.

Jake, Smith, and Claridge continued to crawl forward, with the Afghan tribesman following. The next bodies they reached were dead. Two had been armed, and Smith retrieved another AK-47 from one of them. The next body encountered, however, was the older, white-bearded and white-garbed, man: Fowles' "Elder Dude." He was alive, had a decent pulse, but was unconscious and breathing raggedly. He also bore no apparent wound. Jake reasoned that he may have suffered a heart attack, or even possibly a stroke, and may well have been the man they had heard groaning. Smith and "Younger Dude" began dragging him back to the hut, both still also clutching the rifles that Smith had retrieved. "Younger Dude" occasionally paused to selectively fire back at the enemy.

Jake and Claridge reached the last tribesman, one of the younger men. The clothing over his abdomen was stained a wet red—Jake guessed he'd been gut-shot. He felt for a pulse, and found one—weak—but still a pulse. They began to drag him back toward the hut, Claridge still clutching the confiscated rifle. All the while the bedlam of shelling and rifle fire continued. Just as Jake and the men with him reached the door of the hut, a Taliban fighter, shouldering an RPG launcher, stood up and took aim. Seeing him, Jake figured it was all over. But then the man disappeared in a blast of fire and dirt as an artillery shell scored a direct hit.

Once the SEALs and the three surviving Afghans made it inside the hut, the firing from the Taliban pretty much stopped. The shelling, however, continued unabated, and would continue until Jake called it off, or whenever the helicopters arrived.

As Wilson attended to the two wounded Afghans, Jake and "Younger Dude" conversed (Fowles acting as interpreter). Jake learned that the man was Azzami, eldest son of Azzat, the tribal chieftain. It was Azzat who was the older, white-bearded Afghan in white robes. The third, gut-shot man was Baddar, a nephew, who was a kind of an aide-de-camp to Azzat.

Jake got back on the satellite radio to Conciliation Base, while Fowles and Azzami conversed in Pashto. "Conciliation Base, this is Two-Four Leader. Over."

"Two-Four Leader, this is Conciliation Base. Over."

"This is Two-Four, what is chopper ETA (Estimated Time of Arrival). Over."

"First chopper's ETA approximately twenty, I say again, twenty minutes. Over."

"Roger twenty minutes, Base. Be advised that we have two more wounded Afghan friendlies. Over."

"Roger that, Two-Four. Does Base understand, correctly, that you now have total three wounded? Over."

"Correct, Base. Total three wounded. Over."

"Very well, Two-Four, will advise medevac. Advise current status of Rebel. Over."

"Rebel still okay."

"Roger that. Anything else, Two-Four?"

"Negative, Base. Two-Four Leader, out."

Fowles brought Azzami over to Jake. "L-T," Fowles began, "Azzami here says he can have his fighters here in about fifteen minutes, and he's pretty sure they can send the Tallies packing."

"And how is he going to get them here?" Jake asked.

"Says they're not as primitive as we seem to think. Can you tune to four-six-four point seven megahertz?"

Jake tuned the satellite phone to the requested frequency and handed it to Azzami. The tribesman began transmitting in Pashto. After about a half-dozen exchanges, a self-satisfied looking Azzami handed the radio-telephone back to Jake and spoke to Fowles.

"They're on their way," Fowles reported, translating.

In just thirteen minutes, a cloud of dust appeared from down the highway to the west. Four Toyota light trucks stopped on the roadway and disgorged what seemed to be about three dozen armed men, who fanned out, firing as they ran forward to engage the Taliban.

"Conciliation Base, this is Two-Four Leader. Over."

"Two-Four Leader, this is Conciliation Base. Over."

"This is Two-Four, cease firing. We have friendlies in the area. I say again, artillery to cease firing. Over."

"This is Base, Two-Four, understand artillery to cease firing, friendlies in the area, over."

"That is affirmative, Base, cease firing. Over"

"Roger that, Two-four Leader, Base, out."

By the time Azzami's fellow tribesmen were anywhere near the building, the artillery fire had stopped. Jake, for one, appreciated the new relative quiet.

"Conciliation Base, this is Two-Four Leader. Over."

"Two-Four Leader, this is Base. Over."

"This is Two-Four. Please alert gunship and evac helicopter crews that surrounding area is secured, and not to fire unless fired upon. Over."

"This is Base. Understand area secured? Choppers not to fire unless fired upon? Over." Incredulous.

"That's affirmative, Base. Natives now on ground are friendlies. Choppers are not to fire unless fired upon. Over."

"Roger that, Two-Four. Will pass the word. Conciliation Base, out."

When the Marine helicopters arrived, and judging from the infrequent small arms fire outside the hut, Jake figured that the Taliban had pretty much vacated the area and had fled to the surrounding countryside. Jake was concerned, however, that Conciliation Base had not gotten to the Marines in the choppers on time, warning them not to fire at anyone on the ground who didn't fire at them first.

There were four choppers, total. The two that arrived first were the medevac, a Boeing Vertol, CH-46 Sea Knight, and the attack helicopter gunship, a Bell AH-1Z Viper. The medevac landed just outside the hut, while the Viper remained airborne. The Viper managed to look menacing even while just hovering, and the friendly tribesmen, not wishing to tempt fate, hid themselves as best they could. Apparently, and thankfully, Jake had worried about nothing, and Conciliation Base had successfully conveyed the word to the Marines that they were not to fire unless fired upon; the Viper's guns and missiles remained silent that day.

The three wounded men were loaded quickly aboard the Sea Knight, which then took off straightaway, heading directly for Kandahar Airfield and the NATO Role 3 Multinational Medical Unit there. The Viper flew escort.

Ten minutes later, two Bell UH-1Y Venom light transports arrived, Marine gunners stationed in the doorway.

In the interim, Jake had briefed Longstreet on the role the Afghans had played in the action, and after the Congressman and Jake had shaken hands with Azzami, the SEALs, Longstreet, and the USAID workers took off for Conciliation Base on the Venoms.

A week after the incident, Jake learned that Representative Longstreet had written a letter of commendation for him and his men, and that it had been placed in their personnel files.

Jake never did find out if the school was ever built, but did learn that the two Afghans survived, and were returned home. Likewise, his assistant platoon leader, Lt. j.g. Hank Greenburg, survived, but the incident in Kandahar was, for him, a painful series of surgeries and rehabs in the effort to restore his shattered leg. He was transferred, first, from the MMU to Landstuhl Medical Center in Germany, and then to Bethesda Naval Hospital, in Maryland, for recovery and rehab.

Three weeks and a day after the incident, Jake and his platoon followed Greenburg stateside, their Afghanistan tour completed.

1

Caged

Konarak, Iran

The six Americans were praying together, in verbal communication, even if the three woman couldn't actually see their husbands. It was just as well. Each was filthy, arms and legs covered with blue-black and purple bruises, and those hiding flea bites. Their hair was soiled, greasy, and scraggly. The men had grown unkempt beards. The women wore only the filthy, full-length, orange, baggy dresses. The men only equally-filthy, orange jumpsuits. Yet they thanked God for their having survived another day, and prayed that they would have the strength to endure until He came to their rescue.

Without a window to the outside, and with their jail continuously bathed in bright artificial light, they had no idea how long they had actually been held prisoner. Their communal guess was perhaps a month. It had actually been less than two weeks.

Their prison consisted of two large iron cages, set in a subterranean room with damp concrete walls and floors, and ceilings black with mold. The toilets were buckets in the far corners of each cage. The place stank. It stank of the mold, filthy bodies, and human excrement. Each of them was a banquet for the fleas and lice that lived on them, and, despite the glaring lights, an occasional rat would scud along the walls.

Access to the room, from whatever was outside, was through a single black door of riveted steel plate. The door was beyond the vision of the three women in the cage farthest from it, because the two cages were separated by a cement block wall. The relative cleanliness of the block led the prisoners to conclude that it was of recent construction, its only apparent purpose being to hide the women from the view of the men. While each cage now contained just three prisoners, they were large enough to each hold many more—perhaps as many as fifty—prisoners.

* * * * *

Three months earlier, the *rahbar-e mo'azzam*, or Supreme Leader, of the Islamic Republic of Iran, met with six members of the Guardianship Council in his official residence, the House of Leadership, in the capital, Teheran.

The meeting room was not unlike a corporate board room, with all four walls covered in grey-flocked wallpaper with an indistinct pattern. The Supreme Leader was seated at the head of a long, oval table of polished mahogany. All present wore clerical garb. All sported full beards. The bespectacled Supreme Leader wore a black turban, and a white, ankle-length garment, not unlike the cassocks worn by Christian clergy. Over that, he wore a black-and-white, hounds tooth-patterned prayer shawl, and a long brown smock. The others had chosen the identical white ankle-length cassocks. Over these, they also wore smocks—four of these were black, one cerulean blue, the other a deep maroon—but none of them wore prayer shawls.

Off in a corner, the Supreme Leader's trusted private secretary, Dariush, dressed in just the white cassock-like garment worn over black trousers, and a white, salad-bowl cap, observed and took notes.

The Supreme Leader, in accordance with the Constitution of the Islamic Republic, has essentially dictatorial power over every facet of public life in Iran. He controls the armed forces, the judiciary, state television – in essence, every key governmental agency. The Guardianship Council and the Majlis (or Parliament) are merely advisors to the Supreme Leader. And while the Guardianship Council has the final say in who may or may not run for President, or for a seat in the Parliament, it is the Supreme Leader who appoints the members of the Guardianship Council to begin with. And the Supreme Leader is appointed for life. And 'round and 'round it went. The current Supreme Leader was eighty-two years old, and controlled a personal fortune estimated at ninety-five billion dollars.

"The sitting President of the United States is an avowed enemy of the Iranian people," the Supreme Leader pronounced. The six members of the Guardian Council who were present were the six *faqihs,* or experts in Islamic law, who were, in theory, at least, "conversant with present needs and issues of the day" per the Iranian constitution. (The six members absent were judicial experts, whose advice, this day, was apparently unneeded.)

"The man is a loose cannon," the Supreme Leader continued. "He is an ignorant, orange-haired clown, a devil, and a fool, who is more concerned with self-aggrandizement and disturbing international harmony, than with a peaceful and stable world order." The six Islamic law experts nodded in agreement, but maintained a respectful silence. "His predecessor, at least, was a reasonable man. He could be dealt with. He was perfectly willing to accept our position on peaceful nuclear energy development, and a pause in nuclear weapons development, in return for abolishing the so-called 'sanctions' — those unlawful restrictions to legitimate commerce — imposed on us by the West. He had even convinced all the other major western powers to sign with our Russian ally and accept these terms in a formal agreement." The council members again nodded their assent. They had heard all of this before.

"But this man, this fool American *djinn*," the Supreme Leader continued, "tore up that agreement, and almost convinced the other western nations to do so as well." He paused for effect. "In six months, this devil comes up for reelection. According to the American press, the man's chances for reelection are slim. But the American press also said, four years ago, that the fool would never be elected in the first place. If they were wrong then, they could well be wrong now. The person running against him this time was a member of the previous, more reasonable, regime, and would be infinitely more acceptable to us. We must do whatever we can to see that that person wins election, and that the devil living in the White House does not."

One of the six made ready to speak, and the Supreme Leader nodded to him. "Supreme Leader," he began, "the Russians attempted to influence their last presidential election, and failed. They will most likely try to do so again, and this time, perhaps, be more successful."

The Supreme Leader dismissed his comment with a wave of his hand. "Be that as it may. But we cannot assume that they will do any better than before. I believe they will fail again, because again they will again go about it the wrong way.

We need to provide an embarrassment for this president now —
before the election — an embarrassment from which he cannot
and will not recover.

"Do you recall," he continued, "during the glorious tenure
of my late exalted predecessor, the incident where patriotic
Iranian students overwhelmed the American embassy here in
Teheran, took fifty-two hostages, and held them for four
hundred and forty-four days?"

"Of course, Supreme Leader. Who could ever forget such
an auspicious event?" the same man allowed.

"An event which was not orchestrated by our government,
mind you, but was a free expression of the Iranian people, and
was, in the end, used by our government to its advantage. The
sitting president then was Jimmy Carter, a scold who could
speak only of his own narrow view of morality. *We* brought
him down. We did it then, and we can do it now. All we need
now is a similar incident, a spark, which can then be
exploited."

The assembly fell silent. None of the six dared mention
that the president who followed Carter, dismissed by the world
press as a "grade B movie actor," and by the then Supreme
Leader as an "ignorant dunce," proved to be a far more
formidable obstacle to Iranian foreign policy than Carter ever
was. Eventually, however, one of the six felt impelled to fill the
awkward silence.

"Holiness, an incident on a similar scale involving
Americans will be difficult to produce. Not since 1980 have the
Americans had diplomatic relations with us. There is now no
significant American official presence in Iran. Unless we can
find, and expose, a CIA spy ring, or an American plot to
overthrow the government, or something else of that sort, we
are as tigers without teeth. With no significant American

23

presence in our country, how can there ever be a similar international incident which might succeed in causing this devil to lose the upcoming election?"

"Indeed," the Supreme Leader agreed, "there may be no American diplomatic, and certainly no military, presence in Iran at this time. But there are American visitors coming to Iran *all* the time. Our visa process strives to weed out the troublemakers, and there have thus far been no exploitable incidents involving Americans. But what I propose, and what I will direct the Ministry of Foreign Affairs to do, is this: for the next few months, any American who wishes to visit Iran for any reason whatever will be issued a visa. Then we will keep our eyes open for the right opportunity — any egregiously wrong step by any American, or, better yet, by a group of several Americans — and exploit it. If it is Allah's will that we do this thing, then he will present us with the right opportunity."

And none of the six could argue against such logic.

2

Bringing the Gospel
to the Iranians

Tehran

So much preparation had gone into their mission to the Iranian people! There were all those months of intense study in the Persian language, Farsi, so that they would be able to preach to the people, and answer their questions in their own language. Reading and writing the Persian script had proved to be an impossible task, but, in the end, each of them could engage in an intelligible conversation with anyone else fluent in the Persian language. And the visa process proved to be surprisingly simple. They had expected endless questions as to the purpose of their visit, but there was none of that. Of course, none of them said they were being sent by their congregation to preach the gospel to the heathens. No, they were simple tourists, ordinary Americans wishing to learn the country's customs and immerse themselves in Iranian culture. And that was, after all, *mostly* true.

In Teheran, their actual spreading of the gospel (preaching on the bustling city streets to a smiling, charming, but wary populace), lasted only a few hours. People had politely refused the offered Farsi bibles, holding up their hands and backing away, eyes fearful. Then the men in the in the black uniforms—uniforms that actually had "Police" written on the back in English—came and confiscated their bibles and hauled the six of them off to the Teheran central city jail. They were treated with firm courtesy by the police, although, right from the first, they were separated, the women from the men.

* * * * *

Ehsan, a clerk inside the police station, observed the incident with interest. Long disaffected with the government, he willingly accepted a substantial monthly stipend from the Israeli Intelligence Service (Mossad) in return for whatever information he could pass on (anything at all that might be of interest to his Israeli handler). Whenever he had such information, Ehsan would put it on a thumb drive, and leave it at a blind drop, a location that he knew was checked daily. He had been instructed to use the drop only at such times when he had information to deliver. At any other time, he had been warned to avoid the drop.

It was almost two years ago, Ehsan mused, when he had been recruited. He was in a club, and had had too much to drink, and was telling anyone who would listen that the government, as constituted, was repressive, and that change was long overdue. It was, he proclaimed, time for the young to assert themselves and to take back their country. In the clubs, and generally among Iranian youth, such talk was so common in Teheran that it usually drew no notice whatever. But that night, the clerk drew the attention of an attractive young woman, whose acquaintance he was only too willing to make.

When she heard his boast that he worked for the Teheran police, she set about recruiting him for Mossad. She was *very* attractive, and it took very little convincing and very little time to bring Ehsan into the fold.

He met his handler in person only once, and even then, in almost total darkness. After that, any directive his handler might give him was picked up at yet another blind drop, which he checked daily. He had received no directives in weeks. Other than the location of the blind drops, a shadowy impression of his handler (whom he could identify only as "Ali"), and whatever recollections he might have of the woman who recruited him (long since gone from his life), Ehsan knew nothing. No amount of torture, therefore, however skillfully applied, could get him to reveal what he did not know.

Ehsan recorded the information he had about the American missionaries on a thumb drive, and left it at the blind drop.

The next morning, he picked up this directive: "Keep us informed."

* * * * *

A general order had recently been issued by the Ministry of Foreign Affairs, G.O. number 26379, stating that any incident involving the arrest of Americans was to be immediately reported to *Sāzemān-e Ettelā'āt va Amniyat-e Keshvar*, or SAVAK, the Iranian Organization for National Intelligence and Security. The directive was issued as a "Must Comply — Highest Priority," and failure to obey such a directive would result in serious repercussions. Since the missionaries were American, the incident was, therefore, duly reported by the Teheran police to SAVAK headquarters in the same city.

27

The Americans spent an uncomfortable night as guests of the Teheran police. The next morning, Ehsan checked his blind drop and picked up orders from Ali; his orders this time were more explicit: He was to find out and report in detail whatever he could find out about the Americans.

Later in the day, the errant Americans were reassembled in a large room. Holding court there was a man in a fancy green uniform. Their police escort deferred to him, addressing him as "Colonel," and that is how the missionaries would refer to him forever afterward. The policemen then withdrew, glancing back at the missionaries, their eyes proclaiming genuine compassion.

The colonel wore a neat moustache over a trim beard, his coal-black hair slicked back, and had piercing eyes like polished black glass. He addressed them in a clipped British accent, but he never identified himself.

"Gentlemen and ladies," he began, "let me say that how you answer my questions in the next few minutes will determine whether or not your visit to my country is short, but pleasant, or long, and *very* painful. Your visas say that you are in Iran as tourists. That is obviously a lie. You will now tell me the truth. Why are you here?"

Clayton Rogers spoke up proudly for the group. "We are Evangelical Christian missionaries, here to bring the good news of the Gospel of Jesus Christ to the Iranian people."

"Are you indeed?" the colonel answered, with a tight-lipped smile. "You know, of course—and even if you don't know—that under the law of the Islamic Republic, your preaching constitutes the crime of blasphemy." He paused for effect. "And in this country, a blasphemer is treated as one would treat any traitor. If convicted — and your own admission convicts you — you might well be beheaded."

"We answer to a higher law," Rogers said, only slightly less sure of himself.

The faces of the other five reflected the same self-assurance.

They may very well deport us, Rogers thought, *but certainly they would never execute us. Why ever would they risk an international incident?*

"Perhaps you do, in your country," the colonel said, "but while you are here in Iran you must answer to *our* law."

He gave some kind of signal then, because three men in similar green uniforms (though a bit less fancy) entered the room, handcuffed their wrists behind them, and placed black hoods over the missionaries' heads. They were then brought to another room, and, this time in less-than-perfect English, ordered to sit, and told not to speak. When Clayton Rogers, intending to protest their treatment, began to speak anyway, a guard hit him with something hard across his shins. He cried out in pain. After that, neither Rogers nor anyone else again attempted to speak. *What in the name of God is going on?* Rogers wondered.

The colonel made a call to his immediate superior at SAVAK, and related a synopsis of his interview with the Americans, and what their responses were under his initial interrogation. The colonel was then told to wait, and that his superior would refer the matter to the guardianship council, and then get back to him.

Two hours later, the colonel received a call back from the immediate superior of *his* immediate superior, and was given a set of specific instructions. He knew better than to question his orders, no matter how illogical they seemed. What he *did* know

29

was, that in carrying out the duties of his new assignment, significant obstacles to the successful completion of this newly-assigned mission had just been placed in his path. No matter. He would do his duty nonetheless.

What followed was a whirlwind of activity. After what seemed an interminable wait, sitting in silence and under guard, the Americans, still cuffed and hooded, were unceremoniously shoved into a vehicle of some sort, and driven off.

Any details he could glean about the Americans themselves, and all of the day's activities, were duly noted by Ehsan, the police station clerk. He recorded the information and placed it in his drop box that same evening.

The Americans were driven some distance, and then placed on an aircraft (something they realized only when they sensed it lifting off the ground). Whenever any one of them attempted to speak, he or she would be struck and ordered to be silent.

After seemingly endless hours in the air, the plane landed, and they were taken off and pushed into another vehicle. A long ride followed, and they were then marched down a set of stairs and placed inside a musty-smelling room. They knew they were in a room because they heard a door being locked behind them. When they mustered the courage to speak out, and no blows came, they discovered they were alone.

Sometime afterward, two men entered the room, and the prisoners' hoods and handcuffs were removed. Looking about, they saw they were in a large room; the floor, walls, and ceiling were of poured concrete. The interior was furnished only with a large, rough, wooden table. Speaking heavily-accented and very basic English, the men ordered the prisoners to strip.

When both the men and the women objected, the guards produced telescoping batons and proceeded to beat them, striking each of them indiscriminately. When the guards thought they had inflicted sufficient pain, they ordered the Americans again to take off their clothes, and they had no choice but to do so.

The prisoners, men and women both, were then subjected to a body cavity search by the two men. Then they were given prison uniforms. That meant, for the women, shapeless, orange sackcloth dresses, and for the men, jumpsuits of the same material. These at least covered their otherwise naked bodies.

The next morning, Ehsan, the police station clerk, checking his blind drop, received another directive: "Find out where the Americans have been taken."

3

The House of Leadership

Teheran

The Supreme Leader sat in his private office in the House of Leadership, the official residence of the Supreme Leader of the Islamic Republic of Iran. Apparently, his wardrobe choices were limited, because today he wore one of those same white, cassock-like garments under a black shawl with white trim. He also wore yet another black turban. With him was his secretary, Dariush, who, like himself, was an Islamic theologian. But unlike the Supreme Leader, he was a man totally without guile. Dariush wore a white, salad-bowl cap, and was dressed simply in just an all-white, full-length robe worn over black trousers. Unlike his fully-bearded "boss," he had a wispy, sparse beard and a peach-fuzz moustache.

Dariush was probably the only person in Iran (other than the first of his three wives) whom the Supreme Leader trusted completely. No sycophant, like the twelve ayatollahs on the Guardianship Council, his secretary was intelligent and thoughtful, and could be counted upon to tell the Supreme Leader exactly what he thought—whether or not it was what he wished to hear. And so it was that Dariush frequently made the Supreme Leader angry. It was anger that his boss always regretted upon reflection (a fact that he never would admit to his secretary under any circumstances). But then his anger never seemed to faze Dariush, or elicit any reaction whatever, beyond folded hands and a downward gaze. And that was yet another thing the Supreme Leader liked about the man.

"So, Dariush, it appears that Allah has sent us six American Christian missionaries to do his will."

"If such *is* his will, Supreme Leader. But why transport the Christians from Teheran to a place so remote as Konarak? It would seem that they could be more effectively interrogated right here in Teheran, where SAVAK has facilities much more suited to your—*our*—objectives."

"That is the genius of the plan, Dariush. That such facilities exist in Teheran is well known to our enemies. So it would be perfectly logical to keep the prisoners here. Any attempt to find them, then, to pinpoint their location, and possibly even launch an effort to rescue them, would be concentrated right here in Teheran. So whisk them off quietly and secretly to a place so remote that no one would ever think to look for them there. And Konarak is just such a place."

"But would Konarak even have the facilities to conduct just such an interrogation?" Dariush inquired.

"We have found an ancient prison there that has been appropriated for our purposes, and it should serve us well enough. The situation is obviously not ideal, but the SAVAK Colonel who has been assigned to this operation, is, I am told, very talented. The Director of SAVAK assures me that this Col. Salehrad can make these people actually believe, and freely admit, that they have done anything he tells them that they have done. *And* SAVAK is confident that their man can do this in just six weeks. We will then have more than adequate time left to influence the American election."

"But the world knows, Supreme Leader, that *anyone* can be made to admit to *anything* under duress. And these six, on the face of it, are the most unlikely of spies."

"So the situation is not perfect, I will grant you that much," the ayatollah admitted. "And it is not at all obvious how six street preachers intended to glean our state secrets for the CIA, but it *is* the only opportunity we have at hand. We must work, after all, with the tools Allah gives us."

The secretary smiled. "They are heaven-sent, no doubt. But are they from that boring Christian heaven of harps and chants, or from the heaven of the Garden of a Thousand Delights promised by the Prophet?"

"Say what you mean, Dariush," the Supreme Leader snapped.

"It is as I said, Supreme Leader," Dariush, replied, somewhat cowed. "Six Christian missionaries, people who consider themselves the anointed emissaries of God, would seem to be the most unlikely of CIA agents."

"But wouldn't that be precisely the point?" the Supreme Leader countered. "The CIA would hardly send in people who were *obvious* agents. And who would be less obvious than street preachers?"

"And that is precisely *my* point, Supreme Leader," Dariush gently retorted. "Would you not agree that the Israelis have placed secret agents — *spies* — in our midst?"

Scowling, the Supreme Leader had to admit to himself that such was probably the case.

Having received no response, Dariush continued with his argument. "And how, Holiness, would these Israeli agents, assuming there are such, manage to go undiscovered?"

"I am sure you are about to tell me."

"Well, Holiness, they would be at odds to *not* call attention to themselves . . . to blend in . . . to remain unremarkable, anonymous, unnoticed."

Dariush paused for effect.

"And so it follows," he continued, "that if these Americans were *really* CIA spies, they would hardly be posing as Christian missionaries, preaching their crucified god on a Teheran street corner, and handing out Christian Bibles in the capital of the Islamic Republic. If these people are spies, Supreme Leader, they are undoubtedly the very *unlikeliest* of spies."

The Supreme Leader stayed silent, seeking now his own counsel. His secretary had seen him do this before, and knew enough to now quietly withdraw and leave the ayatollah to his thoughts.

Trust Dariush to highlight the weaknesses in our plan, thought the Supreme Leader. *These particular six Americans are indeed the unlikeliest of spies. But then, the object of the exercise, really, was not to expose the CIA operating in our midst, but to expose the weaknesses of their president's administration. The point of it all is, after all, to embarrass the United States, to make these most unlikely of spies admit publically that, yes, indeed, they are CIA agents. And the half of the world we care about will truly believe it. I do hope that this SAVAK Colonel is every bit the magician his superiors claim him to be.*

The Supreme Leader prayed that this Colonel Farshid Salehrad would succeed. He also prayed most fervently that its current occupant would not spend another four years in the White House.

* * * * *

It took some digging, but Ehsan was finally able to find out where the Americans had been taken. His message that evening to Ali, his handler, was just a single word: "Konarak."'

* * * * *

Later that same evening, Yitzhak Morgenstern, code name "Victor," and known to his Iranian acquaintances as Hamid Alinejad, began driving his 2015 Porche Boxster south from Teheran to Konarak, for a well-earned vacation. He would do some sport fishing in the Gulf of Oman.

4

Prison Life

Konarak

Now, since capture, the missionaries had been given just enough food and water to maintain life and keep them in a constant state of semi-dehydration. They had been allowed to bathe just once thus far, the women apart from the men, in an outside gang shower inside a walled courtyard. Its walls were topped with bright silver concertina wire. The women may not have been allowed to bathe with the men, but they still had to shower in full view of their male jailors. Besides being relieved of their accumulated filth, they were able to see the sun for the first time since their arrest. Once bathed, they were given back the same dirty, and by then, vermin-ridden, clothes they had just removed.

It was unusual that all six were together in the room with the cages at the same time, for their captor's practice was to haul one or two of them from the cages at any one time for interrogation, and then leave them locked in their respective interrogation room for extended periods without food or water.

"Interrogation" could consist of a quiet conversation across the table from the colonel or a "rough" session. Rough sessions placed the subject at the tender mercies of two "interrogation specialists," the same men who had beaten and strip-searched them that first day. Their specialty, apparently, was torture, and they appeared to relish their work. These men, one heavyset, tall, and bald, the other, shorter, wiry, and hairy, were called, respectively, "Screwtape" and "Wormwood" by the missionaries (after the two devils in C.S. Lewis' *The Screwtape Letters*).

Physical beatings were frequent enough, and none of the missionaries still had their toenails. Waterboarding was also used, but electric shock was Screwtape's and Wormwood's favorite. Subjects were bound, naked, suspended by their wrists by leather straps from above, and standing in galvanized tubs filled with water. Electric current was then passed through electrodes clamped to their genitals. The electrical circuit could be broken only by the subject hoisting himself up by his wrists and lifting his or her feet out of the water. They could, of course, hold this position for only so long, and when their strength gave out, and when their toes once again touched the water . . .

Screwtape and Wormwood never ceased to be amused by this macabre dance.

For the three women, a rough interrogation might also include rape, on occasion by both men in the same session. But Screwtape and Wormwood never sexually assaulted the men. Such activity was, after all, explicitly forbidden in the Quran. Indeed, the Hadith prescribes the death penalty for such behavior. And both Screwtape and Wormwood were devout Muslims.

The colonel was careful never to be present at any of the rough interrogations.

And interrogation across the table from the colonel was infinitely more preferable. The colonel always spoke to the prisoners in his clipped, perfect English, and always seemed to be genuinely concerned about the captives. Polite conversation always eventually led to the American's purpose in visiting Iran, and they were gently encouraged to confess their crimes. If only they would admit that they were American spies who had infiltrated Iran to discover state secrets, then, and only then, he assured them, would all the ill treatment cease. If they only told the "truth," he assured them, they would be clean, well-treated, and well fed.

The three American couples never denied that they were Evangelical Christian missionaries come to Iran in order to spread the Gospel and convert Muslims. They freely owned up to this particular "crime" to their captors. Thus far, however, no one would admit to being a spy for the CIA or any other agency of the United States. Indeed, one of the women did indeed have a secret, one that only her husband shared. It was a secret that would, no doubt, be of great interest to her interrogators, but the couple had, thus far, managed to keep from them.

The Iranian News Agency, ISNA, had released the information on their capture and detention, but had thus far only published a group picture of the six "CIA spies," dressed in their shapeless orange prison uniforms, and had provided no other details besides their names. The story of the couples' detection and capture that the agency released was made up out of whole cloth. Promised details as to the spies' mission and motives would be made public only when they became available, and the spies were ready to publicly proclaim their repentance for having tried to "infiltrate and disrupt" the governance of the Islamic Republic. It was for that end – a public admission of guilt—that the colonel and his men were working. But, thus far, none of the six had cracked.

Nonetheless, the torture was taking its toll, and now the six prayed for the grace to resist.

5

Hamid

Konarak

Hamid Alinejad, code name "Victor," arrived in Konarak after a 20-hour, 1,600 km drive over some rough roads. It was late evening, and he drove around town, taking the measure of the place. As it happened, he passed by a hotel on the southern end of town and saw a fancy, late-model Mercedes luxury SUV parked outside. On a hunch, he parked his own car, and went inside, striking up a conversation with the desk clerk.

"My name is Hamid Alinejad. I am here on vacation, and am planning to do some sport fishing," he informed the clerk. The clerk wore European-cut brown suit, blue dress shirt and a solid maroon tie.

"Yes, *Sir*," the clerk replied, taking the measure of the man in front of him: impeccably-groomed, sharply creased dark blue slacks, an Italian-tailored silk sport shirt of a lighter blue hue. "Konarak is famous for some of the best fishing in the world."

"So I have heard. I am looking for place to stay during my visit—a base of operations, more or less, convenient to the marina."

"We are as close as any other hotel in town," the clerk said, smiling. "And the only reason we have so few guests at the moment," he assured his prospective guest, "is that it is off-season. But I can assure you, Mr. Alinejad, that all our facilities are first class. Our restaurant, for example, is among the best in the city. I would be happy to show you one of our rooms, if you wish."

"Well," Hamid replied, "I was thinking more in terms of a suite. On your top floor, perhaps—for the view of the Gulf?"

The clerk frowned. "As fortune would have it, Sir, the third-floor suite with the view to the Gulf is occupied. The second-floor suite just below it is available, however, and it also has an excellent view of the Gulf. But if you prefer to be on the third floor, Sir, then the suite at the opposite end of the third floor is available. I would be happy to show you either suite. And I can assure you, Mr. Alinejad, our off-season rates are quite reasonable."

"I suppose the owner of the fancy Mercedes parked outside is in the third-floor suite with the Gulf view?"

"He is, Sir." The clerk smiled, and then continued. "And a very important man he is. He is a colonel with the Iranian Intelligence Service. A very important man, Sir. Colonel Farshid Salehrad."

"I would imagine then that he *is* an important man. Is he also here for the sport fishing?"

"Oh no, sir, he is not, I am afraid. The central government owns a facility—an old prison, really, dating back to the shahs—just outside of the city. It used to be just a spot for the tour guides to show the tourists. I have been on one such tour myself. You know, 'Qajar prison, former center of torture for the shah and his corrupt and repressive regime,' that sort of thing. But now the colonel and his men have taken the place over. Nobody is exactly sure why, but it's for certain that SAVAK wants it reactivated for the good of the Republic.

"But the place is very small, and very dirty. It is also run down, and *very* depressing. It has not been used as a jail or anything else other than a tourist attraction for decades . . . May I show you one of the suites now, Mr. Alinejad?"

"How interesting. But would you say that this place— Qajar prison, was it?—is now off limits to tourists?"

The clerk nodded his assent. "Oh yes, Sir. Very much so. Aside from Colonel Salehrad and his men, the only people now allowed to go near the place are the two townswomen they've hired to cook and clean for the colonel's men."

"Cook and Clean? But then his men must be staying at the place. How come the colonel doesn't stay there as well?"

"Well, Mr. Alinejad, it's obviously because the colonel is a gentleman. The facilities at the prison for the staff—remember I have been on a tour of the place and have seen them—are not much better than the cages in the basement where the shahs used to keep their prisoners! No, Sir, I can assure you the colonel much prefers to stay here. And so will you, Mr. Alinejad, of that I am quite sure. May I *please* show you one or both of the available suites?"

"Well, if this hotel is good enough for such an important man . . ." he chuckled, "show me the second-floor suite."

After making a show of examining the proffered suite, Hamid checked into the hotel, but only after the clerk had been assured that payment would be made in euros.

6

The White House

Washington, D.C.

The pastor of the Church of the Good News in Farmington, Mississippi, notified his close friend, and the state's most influential congressman, the Honorable Robert Longstreet, just three days after he had lost touch with the six missionaries his congregation had sent into Iran. The pastor (unlike the rest of his congregation) also knew that Rep. Longstreet had a very special relationship with one of the couples now gone missing. His daughter, the former Clare Longstreet, and her husband, John Tindal, were one of the couples abducted. The congressman, the pastor noted, was at once very concerned and agitated over the matter, and promised, to the pastor's immense satisfaction, immediate and effective action. The congressman lost no time in taking the matter up with the state department, which, in its turn, had agreed to launch an inquiry into the matter through the Swiss Embassy in Teheran. In the interim, IRNA, the official news agency of the Islamic Republic of Iran, had announced the arrest of six American spies who had entered the country but had provided only scant details.

IRNA had not, as yet, publicly identified the detainees beyond publishing the group picture and simply listing their names.

On noting this, Rep. Longstreet knew it was only a matter of time before his daughter and son-in-law's true identity became public, and decided he couldn't wait for the state department to act; he asked for an immediate audience with the president. Meanwhile, the president had been updated by the secretary of state on the hostage situation, and, because of the Mississippi connection, suspected the reason for Longstreet's request.

* * * * *

The president's secretary announced the visitor on the intercom.

"Representative Longstreet to see you, Sir."

"Okay, Louella, send him in."

Robert Longstreet opened the door to the oval office warily, and peered in. He wore an open-collared white shirt under his suit jacket, and, uncharacteristically, the suit jacket and trousers were rumpled. To the president, who was there to meet him at the door, he appeared tired and worn out. Longstreet knew the president well, having campaigned with him throughout Mississippi during the election, but had never before requested a private audience with the man. But, then, he had never had his daughter locked up in an unfriendly country, before, either.

"Come in, Bob, come in!" the president invited, cordially. The president was dressed casually, in mauve golf slacks and a matching polo shirt. Longstreet entered the room and the president shook his hand warmly, then pointing to a chair. The president couldn't help but note that Longstreet, normally a very calm, cool, and collected individual, was today acting very disturbed and agitated.

"Sit down, Bob," he said, "You look like you've had better days. Much better days,"

Longstreet sat down stiffly in the chair the president had pointed to. He was surprised when the president sat down next to him, rather than behind his massive polished mahogany desk.

"Right. Now, Bob, what can I do for you?"

"Pretty sure you know why I'm here," Longstreet began, his voice strained, but firm and steady.

"Yes, I'm pretty sure I do. Scary thing, Bob, those missionaries from your state being in this situation."

Longstreet had expected him to continue along the lines of "What could those idiots have been thinking; putting themselves in that position," but instead heard:

"And I'm not going to sugar-coat it for you, Bob. The Iranians are not our friends. No, Bob, they're not. Definitely *not* our friends. And they are a very nasty bunch. Really nasty. But I want you to know I'm gonna do everything I can, Bob, everything I can. I'm going to pull out all the stops — *all* the stops — to bring them home . . . every last one of them."

"I appreciate that, Sir, I really do." Emboldened, he said, "But I have some information that will definitely complicate the situation even more. "

"You do? And what's that, Bob?"

"One of the couples, Mr. President, Clare and John Tindal. They're my daughter and son-in-law."

"Holy shit, Bob!" the president exclaimed, his face registering complete shock and surprise. The conversation ceased for a minute, as Longstreet let the information sink in.

Finally, the president said: "That does complicate things. It really does!"

After another pause, the president spoke again. "But I meant what I said before, Bob, and I still really mean it: I will do everything I can to bring them home. Every last one of them. Your daughter and son-in-law included. *All* of them, Bob."

"Thank you, Mr. President. I know you will and I greatly appreciate that.

"And I know," Longstreet continued, "that you have to hit the Iranians on the diplomatic front first. But you and I both know, Mr. President, that that's probably a dead end.

"Please, Sir, I want—no, I *need*—your assurance, that, if need be, you won't hesitate to send in a SEAL team in after my daughter and the rest of them!"

Now the president had to choke back a chuckle. "A SEAL team, Bob? Not the Marines or Delta Force? The SEALs, Bob?"

Longstreet held his ground. "Nothing less, Sir. Not that I have anything against the Marines or Delta Force for that matter, but it was the SEALs that saved my ass in Afghanistan, and, if it's at all possible, and I'd appreciate it, Sir, that if you send anybody in, you send in SEALs."

If the president was even slightly amused by Longstreet's vehemence, or was goading him, he didn't let on. "Any particular SEAL team you have in mind, Bob?"

Longstreet's face suddenly lit up, as if a terrific idea had just come to him. "If you can, Mr. President, the exact same SEAL team that pulled out my ass in Afghanistan!"

"Names, Bob? Who were these SEAL guys?"

"Well, the team leader was a Navy Lieutenant named Lawlor—Jake Lawlor."

"Like the Admiral? Wazizname? J.J. Lawlor?"

47

"His son."

"Well, Bob, if that can be arranged, and if we do have to send people in after your daughter and the others, I'll do my best to see we send in Lawlor and his SEAL team. Assuming, of course, it's at all possible!"

Longstreet looked genuinely relieved.

"Thank you, Sir!"

* * * * *

After alerting both men on the phone that same morning of the latest development in "the Iran situation," the president met with the secretary of state and the secretary of defense in the oval office later that day. (The office had been newly decorated by the president's third wife, the former fashion model. The walls were now eggshell white, and the wood trim robin's egg blue.) The president was dressed in the same mauve polo shirt and matching slacks he wore earlier. The other two men were dressed in dark-colored business suits (indigo or black—it was hard to tell), with white shirts and ties of subdued hues.

"What the hell are we going to do about this?" the president asked his advisors. "The Evangelicals are breathing down my neck, and worse, Bob Longstreet, one of my biggest and most effective boosters in the House, is understandably up in arms over this thing. As you now both well know, his daughter and her husband are one of the couples involved. If the Iranians know this, they sure as hell have kept quiet about it. They haven't even identified these people publicly beyond listing their names. Not yet, anyway. No doubt they're scheming to release any information so that it will do major damage to our interests in the region, and maximize its effect on the election. No secret they would just love to see me lose.

They're out to screw me. Screw me, yes, and this whole thing could blow up in my face. Lousy situation, lousy.

"I can't afford to lose the Evangelical vote, can't afford that. *And* if we can't get these people out of Iran, I could very well lose the respect of the entire American voting public and be out of a job in January!"

The secretary of state, Harrison Fielding (a Princeton graduate, who looked more like a college professor than the successful businessman he was before the president tapped him for his cabinet) intoned, "It's not just Bob Longstreet, or even the Evangelicals, Mr. President. You're dead right. The real reason behind this incident is the election—*period*. The Iranians want to embarrass the United States, but they want to embarrass *you* in particular. They want you to appear weak and ineffective. They want to discredit you and see to it you don't get reelected.

"And as far as the six missionaries are concerned," he continued, "just their preaching Jesus to the Iranian public is a violation of Sharia law—which is pretty much the law of the land in the Islamic Republic. But from what little detail IRNA has reported, we don't even know if they've already admitted to that. But getting missionaries to admit they're missionaries shouldn't be that hard to do. So, if they wanted to, the Iranians could easily just convict them of attempting to subvert Islam and, if they had a mind to, even behead them for it. But the ayatollahs apparently want more than that. They are claiming that the detainees are also spies for the United States, and they mean to get these poor bastards to confess to that, *and* to embarrass the United States in general, and you, Mr. President, in particular.

"One thing might be working in our favor, though," he went on, "Apparently, and for whatever reason, the ayatollahs

49

haven't found out that the woman, Clare Tindal, is Bob Longstreet's daughter. Surely, if they knew that, they'd have run with it long since."

"Well, maybe they haven't found out yet," the president agreed, "But it's only a matter of time before some asshole from one of the news agencies finds out and spills the beans. Damn media! Out to get me. They've been after my ass from the get-go! Soon as they found out I'd been elected! And I haven't exactly made it a secret that I don't trust those Iranian bastards . . . Okay then. How about you people? Do you really think they can use this thing, and influence the election enough to make me lose?"

"Well, Sir," Fielding replied, "didn't they do precisely that to Jimmy Carter in 1980? The Iranian embassy crisis did as much to lose the election for Carter as anything else. Make no mistake, Mr. President, the ayatollahs want you to lose this election, and they want your opponent to win. They want someone weak and ineffective in office, someone exactly like the geriatric holdover from the last administration running against you—someone who'll gut the military to pay for the social programs that jerk's party is pushing—someone who would never have pulled out of that nuclear arms deal. Your pulling out of the agreement and ramping up sanctions was, you know, to them, an unforgivable sin."

The president scowled. "That was a lousy deal, Harry, even though you fought me like hell on the pullout. A definitely lousy deal. Terrible. All my predecessor did with that deal was take the immediate pressure off the Iranians to kill their nuclear weapons program and then kick that can down the road . . .

"But this isn't solving the problem at hand." He paused. "You know, these six Evangelicals, they really irritate me," he said, having changed his train of thought. "What in hell were they thinking going in there like that in the first place? Do these people even speak Arabic, or whatever language the Iranians speak?"

"Farsi," Fielding advised.

"What?"

"The Iranians speak Farsi, Mr. President, and apparently, at least according to their pastor, the missionaries are fluent in that language."

"Whatever. But what does Iran expect to gain by arresting *these* poor *schleps*? How can they possibly expect to convince the world these religious kooks are actual spies, even if one of them is related to a congressman?"

"His *daughter*, Sir."

"Okay. There's that. But even so."

"By having them admit to being spies, *publicly*." interjected Gordon Jones, the secretary of defense, a former Marine major general. "Rest assured, Mr. President, given time, the Iranians will eventually break these people. In time, *everybody* breaks. And then, to a man, they'll say that they were spies and whatever else they're told to say. I'm actually surprised they haven't broken them already and paraded them in front of the cameras. Then I think they'll put the poor bastards on trial—an old Soviet-style trial—and they'll be convicted and sentenced to whatever . . . maybe even beheading.

"But," Jones continued, "if they just convicted them of proselytizing Christianity and then gave them harsh sentences, the British and the European Union would complain like hell, and the Iranians would have to back down. After all, Iran wants the Brits and the Frogs and the rest of our allies to keep buying their oil. But if they ever find out that Clare Tindal is Bob Longstreet's daughter, and can get the missionaries to confess to being spies, then the Brits and the EU, while perhaps not buying that they're actual spies, still wouldn't scream near as loud. And the Iranians know full well that every dinky country in the Mideast — except maybe Israel — *will* buy it. So even if they don't make you lose the election, they come out ahead no matter what."

"I get it," the president said. "I get it . . . Harry, I do. But do we have *any* diplomatic options — any at all?"

"There's not much we can do diplomatically, Mr. President," Fielding admitted. "We don't even have diplomatic relations with Iran, not since 1980, and so we'll have to work through the Swiss, and that only complicates things. We've been trying to get the Swiss ambassador, or the Red Cross, or the Red Crescent, or the U.N., or *somebody* in there to see these people and ensure they're being treated humanely. But the Iranians have stonewalled us and everybody else. They won't tell the Swiss, or the U.N., or anyone else, a damned thing other than that they're holding six Americans as spies, and that the six Americans are being treated as such."

"That's crap," the president said, musing aloud. "Pure bullshit. Why would anyone in their right mind believe that we'd use six religious ding-dongs to spy on Iran, even if one of them *is* related to Bob Longstreet? Hell, Longstreet sits on the House *Education and Labor* Committee, for shit's sake! That committee's not even remotely related to national security!"

He paused once again to collect his thoughts when Fielding interjected, "And he's House Minority Whip, Sir."

"What?"

"Longstreet, Sir, he's also House Minority Whip."

"House Minority Whip? Shit, Harry, I'll bet there aren't thirty people in this whole country, outside of the House, who know what in hell that is. And I'm including all hundred

Senators!" Another pause, but this time nobody interrupted his train of thought.

"And what the hell kind of spy cover is that, anyway, sending in Christian missionaries to convert Muslims? Even the Iranians can see how stupid that is!"

He then eyed the two men sharply, first Fielding, then Jones. "No, you're right. They're doing this to embarrass me, make me look weak to the Iraqis and the Syrians and the rest of the Muslim countries. It's just politics — pure bullshit politics."

The secretary of state looked glum, and said, "People around the world will believe what they want to believe."

The president turned to the secretary of defense, who had thus far been relatively quiet. "How about the military, Gordy? You're a General. Any way your people can get them out before the Iranians can capitalize on this?"

"An operation like that could take months to set up," Jones answered, his bearing military, even seated. "Hell, we don't even know for sure where these people are being held. We can be damn sure the Iranians will be expecting us to try something like that — and they *will* be waiting for us."

"Are you saying it would be impossible?" the president asked, pursing his lips and lowering his eyebrows the way he did. "Because I don't want to hear that. I don't. And I don't want to hear 'months,' either. From what we already know, we've got days, maybe weeks, but definitely not months, to fix this. The Iranians will have them convicted, and maybe even beheaded, while we're still sitting here, playing with ourselves. Playing with ourselves!"

Again, the president sat silent for a few moments, looking pensive. The other two men had seen this particular look before. They knew that they were about to get their marching orders. "Okay," he said finally, "America deserves action. Bob

Longstreet deserves action—and I want action, and I want it *quick."* His eyes moved from one to the other, making sure that both knew he expected them to find a solution to the problem, diplomatic, military, or otherwise. "Both of you get with your troops and see what we can do. But we *will* use any means necessary to get those people out of there, and damn soon! Damn soon!"

"Yes. Mr. President," they said in unison. Then the two men moved to leave the oval office quickly, but the president motioned for Jones to stay behind.

"Gordy, Bob Longstreet is a special friend, and he made a special request. I'd like you to honor it, if you can."

"Sir?"

"If we *do* decide to send in a rescue team, he's asked that it be the same guys that saved his ass in Afghanistan."

"Which guys, Sir?"

"SEALs, Gordy, SEALs. A SEAL team led by Admiral Lawlor's son. He's a Lieutenant, I think Bob said."

"Yes Sir, that can be arranged, just so long as the head of Navy Special Ops, Admiral Williams, goes along with it. Ultimately, Lawlor works for him."

"And Willaims works for you. So see to it that he does, Gordy. Goes along with it. *You're* in charge."

"Yes Sir, Mr. President."

That evening, a tweet: @*POTUS: Cowardly Iranians holding six innocent American citizens on bogus charges! Rest assured; we will get them out! And soon!*

The Supreme Leader was delighted when news of the president's tweet was reported to him. *Perhaps, despite the flimsiness of the charges we can bring against these hapless Americans,* he thought, *the president of the United States himself can turn this incident into one of major international implications.* He chuckled, pleased with himself. *The fool himself will provide the very sword with which we shall strike off his head!*

And then CNN broke the story that one of the missionaries accused of spying on Iran for the CIA, Mrs. Clare Tindal, was the daughter of Mississippi Representative Robert Longstreet, House Minority Whip, and one of the president's staunchest supporters in the House of Representatives. Soon the story was running on all the wire services, and reported by all the major media outlets.

7

Defining the Problem

Washington, D.C.

The DOD building in northwest Washington, D.C., is a grey, granite-block edifice located at the convergence of 16th Street with both Massachusetts and Rhode Island Avenues. There, Gordon Jones, the secretary of defense, met with Helen Siebert, the president's national security advisor, and Charles Cuthbert, the director of the CIA. Cuthbert was a career bureaucrat, who had risen through the administrative ranks at CIA, and had only briefly served as a field operative.

Helen Siebert's presence at the meeting was, on Jones' part, just a matter of courtesy. It was no secret that Jones had little regard for her, but the president really liked the diminutive black woman he'd appointed as his national security advisor. Siebert was, as far as Jones was concerned, just another ivory-tower academic, this time out of Stanford, who, like Jones himself, had never held an elective office. But unlike Jones, she had also never been in the military and led troops, nor run a business, nor had to meet a payroll. On the other hand, Siebert had served in advisory posts in three previous administrations. She was also an accomplished pianist, who could just as easily have had a career on the concert stage, had she not chosen one in academia and public service. But, despite her impressive résumé, Jones still considered Siebert just another overbearing busybody with a Ph.D.

"Charles, Ms. Siebert," Jones began, "I'm sure that you're aware of the problems we're faced with. Obviously, the president's tweet last night wasn't very helpful. Worse, the media couldn't wait to connect one of the missionaries with a sitting U.S. congressman, and one of the president's biggest allies. No, the tweet was the least of it. The president really didn't say anything specific, anyway, other than we'll be trying to get these people back — and I'm sure the Iranians had already figured on that. But the other thing is *murder*. The daughter of a sitting congressman arrested in Iran for spying. That will raise a real shit storm. The thing is, what in blazes do we do about it?

"Now," Jones continued, "Assuming diplomatic efforts fail — and the chances of their succeeding, especially now, are slim — then we will be expected to extract the detainees from Iran by force, and the Iranians will be expecting just that and *will* be waiting for us. And obviously the last thing we want is a repeat of the 1980 U.S. Embassy hostage rescue fiasco. Now I realize that operation failed because of military screw-ups and equipment failure, but at least we knew where our people were being held, right down to the room they were being held in. In this case, we've got nothing. *Nada*. We can only assume that our people are still somewhere in Teheran, but we don't even know *that* for sure. We *desperately* need some intel. So what can you guys do for me?"

Charles Cuthbert was a Georgetown grad, with a degree in political science. His hair resisted his every effort to comb it, and it stuck out in all directions. Nearsighted, he wore glasses

57

with thick black rims, these perched on a bulbous nose. Cuthbert sported a business suit almost identical in color to the one Jones wore, but it was crumpled and ill-fitting. He somehow, however, always managed looked pensive and intelligent.

"We've got nothing at CIA," he admitted. "Our Iranian assets are sparse to begin with, and nobody on the ground there seems to know anything. They've been told to keep digging, but thus far the prospect for any real intel looks grim."

"That's not at all what I'd hoped to hear," said Jones. The disappointment in his voice was palpable.

Helen Siebert, looking pretty, yet very businesslike, in a tailored, gray pants suit, spoke up. "What about the Israelis? I can almost guarantee they have a greater presence there than we do, or anybody else, for that matter. Have you tried reaching out to them?"

"No," Cuthbert admitted. "I thought that maybe we should try talking to the Saudis first."

"*Screw* the Saudis!" Siebert spat out. Both men were taken aback at the vehemence expressed in her outburst. "They're the *last* people I would consult! Don't ever forget that Bin Laden and sixteen out of the nineteen 9/11 hijackers were *all* Saudis. Get them involved, and ten minutes later all our enemies in the Middle East will know exactly what we're up to. No, you need to talk to our *real* ally in the Middle East—our *only* ally there, truth be told—talk to the Israelis."

"Yes, ma'am," Cuthbert, cowed, replied. He glanced at Jones, and saw the look of pleasant surprise on his face.

"She's right, Charlie," he said. He turned to her smiling, "You're exactly right, Helen!"

"I'll get right on it," Cuthbert said.

8

Regrouping

Konarak

The six missionaries were huddled together in the corners of their cages that were closest to the block wall, the one that separated the men from the women. Three pairs of hands were interlocked, having reached around the end of the cement block wall. They spoke in whispers, just loud enough to be audible to each other. They had become understandably very paranoid, and were sure the Iranians had bugged their cages and were recording their every word.

"Surely they must know we speak Farsi," Adele Crowley whispered, "Screwtape and Wormwood talk to us in English—their version of it, anyway—and the colonel questions us only in English, but he speaks to his men only in Farsi, as if he thought we couldn't understand a word he was saying."

"Well, that's because the others probably don't know any English. Do you think the colonel really *doesn't* know we understand Farsi?" her husband Justin asked, gently squeezing her hand.

"How could he not?" she answered. "What good would it do if we preached to Iranians in English? No one would understand us. He can't be that stupid. It's all just part of the crazy game they're playing with us. Anything to keep us off balance."

"Of course," opined John Tindal. "Surely the Colonel knows we understand him when he speaks Farsi. Maybe he just doesn't care. Or, more likely, just as Justin says, he's playing us — just another way of messing with our heads."

"I think you're both right, John," agreed Adele Crowley, "you and Justin. He's just messing with our heads. I specifically heard the Colonel, in Farsi, telling the guards to remind Screwtape that when he or Wormwood beat us . . ." Her husband groaned, deeply disturbed at the thought of his wife being beaten.

Adele breathed deeply, and continued. "He told him not to touch our faces, to hit us only where the bruises wouldn't be seen on camera. And I don't think he cared if I knew that." Her husband again groaned. "Don't, Justin," she said. "We must have courage. Remember that I suffer — we *all* suffer — for Christ."

"I *do* know that," Justin said, "and for myself, I do so willingly. But the thought of you being tortured breaks my heart," he sobbed.

If you only knew the half of it, Adele thought.

None of the women had told the men what had been done to them beyond the beatings, the waterboarding, and the electric shocks. But what the women didn't know, was that Screwtape and Wormwood had boasted of the pleasure their wives had afforded them, as part of their methodical torture of their husbands. Their husband's silence was the only way they could spare their wives even more pain.

"Courage," intoned Clayton Rogers, a church elder and the group's leader. "But now that I think about it, you're right,

Adele, they haven't touched *my* face either, and I can see now that neither have they touched Justin's or John's. Mary and Clare, have they hurt your faces?"

"No, they haven't," Mary Rogers spoke for herself and Clare Tindal.

"Obviously, if they don't want to mar our faces, it's because they can then parade us before the cameras looking as if we weren't coerced to confess our 'crimes' to the world," Clayton said. "Probably some kind of show for the world press, no doubt. But think about it . . . the colonel is sending us a subtle message, isn't he? Give in to him, let him break us, and all that will happen is that we will be paraded in front of the cameras, we'll confess our sins, and then we'll be well treated — they *may* even let us go home. And isn't that what he keeps promising in those calm interrogation sessions of his? Just confess, and all the pain will stop? Oh, the man must be ever so confident he will break us! All the more reason for us not to give in!"

"But I'm so hungry, and tired, and filthy," Clare Tindal complained, as she scratched at a flea bite. "And sore. My poor body is *so* sore. And my poor, ripped-apart toes are aflame. Please pray for me. I don't know how much longer I can hold out." She had told no one her secret, and, except for her husband and their pastor, none of the others ever knew who her father was. She had always considered it a sin of pride to play on her father's reputation, and, even in college, she had kept, as much as she could, her father's identity moot. What she didn't know was that, other than her fellow missionaries, the whole world now not only knew who she was, but also who her father was.

"Courage, Clare," Clayton Rogers intoned again. "We are all likewise suffering. We must pray for each other. Always.

And remember that it is the cross of suffering that is the symbol of our salvation. We suffer for Christ. And we *must* trust in God."

But nobody answered "Amen."

Then two guards came into the room. They unlocked the women's cage and dragged Adele Crowley and Clare Tindal out. Relocking the cage, they handcuffed each and put black hoods over their heads. As the guards marched the women out of the room, Clare Tindal was sobbing uncontrollably.

9

Conference Call

Washington, D.C., and Tel Aviv, Israel

Charles Cuthbert had Helen Siebert place the call on a secure line to Tel Aviv. He knew that she and Shlomo Rosenszweig, the head of the Israeli National Intelligence Agency (Mossad), were close, so Cuthbert insisted she join in on the call. Siebert needed very little convincing, and readily agreed to place the call to her old friend.

"Moe, it's Helen."

"Hello, Helen, how nice to hear from you!"

"Moe, I have Charlie Cuthbert on the line with us."

"Ah . . . an official call, then. Hello, Charles."

"Good morning, Sir," Cuthbert replied.

"Moe," he corrected. "Call me Moe. I am correct, Helen, am I not? This is an *official* call?" Rosenszweig asked.

"Cut the crap, Moe," Siebert said, "you know *exactly* why we're calling."

Rosenszweig chuckled. "Straight for the jugular, as always, eh, Helen? I am glad to see you are feeling well, and are your old self! I can assume, then, it is about your new hostage crisis in Iran? Now, how can I help you?"

Cuthbert spoke up. "We're blind, Sir—err, Moe—totally blind," he admitted. "Our assets on the ground there are thin, and we don't even have a clue where our people are being held."

"I can tell you that. They are in Qajar prison, in a city called Konarak, in the southeast corner of the country."

Surprised, the Americans took a second to let this new information sink in.

"But they were arrested in Teheran, and that's all the way to the north," Cuthbert said, still surprised.

"Of course, they were. And the Iranians figured that if you were looking for them, you would be looking there. So they flew them 1,600 kilometers south to hide them, keeping you off the scent."

"And this prison, K-jar, what can you tell us about that?" Cuthbert asked.

"Nothing at the moment, other than it is named after one of their former shahs. But we'd be willing to look into it for you." (Actually, since the six Americans were arrested, Rosenszweig knew very well that his people had already been scrambling for as much information as they could gather. Information, was, after all, currency.)

"You're not holding out on us, Moe, are you?" Siebert asked, knowing the man.

"Heavens, no, Helen," Rosenszweig chuckled, "not this time, at least."

"All right, then," she said, "when can you give us more intel, Moe? We need to get these people out, and fast."

"Ah, yes," Rosenszweig replied, "there *is* an election coming up. As soon as I know more, you will also."

When the call was completed, Cuthbert and Siebert scrambled to find a map of Iran, to find out exactly where this Konarak was.

10

Little Creek, Virginia

Lieutenant Jacob Joseph Lawlor, Jr., was OIC (Officer in Charge) of the Fourth Platoon, SEAL Team Two, headquartered in Little Creek, Virginia. Lawlor was third generation Navy. He graduated from the Naval Academy in 2012, the third person in his family to do so, after his father and grandfather.

His grandfather, the late Jacob Julius Lawlor, fought in submarines in WWII, was highly decorated (five Navy Crosses), and had survived a dozen war patrols. He had retired as COMSUBLANT (Commander, Submarine Forces, Atlantic) in the '80s, with the rank of Vice Admiral.

Jake Junior's dad, Jacob *Joseph* "J.J." Lawlor, Sr., had followed in *his* father's footsteps and also joined the submarine service. There, he rose to command the diesel-electric boat *Cuttlefish,* and the nuclear-powered boats *Conch, Long Beach,* and *Thomas A. Edison.* After promotion to Rear Admiral, J.J. was given his present job in the Navy Department, as Director of Underwater Unmanned Vehicles Development.

Jake Junior had somewhat disappointed his forebears by eschewing the submarine service to join the Navy SEALs (Sea-Air-Land). Having originally been counted among the roughly twenty percent of applicants to survive the grueling BUDS training regimen at the Naval Amphibious Base in Coronado, California, he was now a platoon leader in SEAL Team Two.

At six-foot three inches, Jake was the tallest male in his family. And, like his relatively diminutive grandfather and only slightly taller father, he was powerfully built, his body toned by daily strenuous training and hours on end spent on the running track and in the weight room.

Jake's hair was brownish-blond, worn close-cropped, high and tight, with Marine-style "white sidewalls." Jake's father (like his grandfather) had married a fair-skinned Irish Catholic, and Jake had inherited her ice-blue eyes.

Woman usually found Jake's chiseled, clean-cut good looks attractive. But, although there had been a couple of somewhat-serious dating relationships, Jake, now twenty-nine years old, remained single. And he felt obligated to stay that way. After all, he knew that what he did was dangerous, and, like that firefight in Afghanistan, he may well not survive the next such incident. Hell, even *routine* SEAL training was dangerous! No, Jake felt he had no right to ask a woman—any woman—to live like that: always worrying that her husband might not survive his next mission. But he had met a young lady—about, what, nine months ago, was it?—who had made him question his resolve.

Now, again, something was up. Word had come down from on high that Jake and the senior enlisted man in his platoon, Chief Petty Officer William Cole, were to appear at the team commander's office at 1400 sharp. Cole, an African-American with almost classically Grecian good looks, was every bit as powerfully built as Jake. Unlike Jake, however, Cole, at thirty-one, he was married and the father of two. Apparently, Cole had no such reservations about at once being a SEAL *and* a family man. The two men had served together since Jake assumed command of the SEAL platoon, trusted each other implicitly, and had become best friends, even to the point of being on a first name basis in private. A third person would also have been directed to attend, Jake's assistant platoon leader, Lt. j.g. Henry "Hank" Greenburg, but he was in the Bethesda Naval Hospital, recovering from a series of operations to restore a shattered femur. Greenburg had been on tap to take over Jake's platoon, with Jake scheduled to move up to staff, but Hank's injury had put that plan on at least a temporary hold. Not that Jake was looking forward to a staff assignment, anyway.

At precisely 1400, Jake, with Cole in tow, knocked on the team commander's door.

"Enter," was heard, and the two men opened the door, walked into the office of Commander Harold Porter, and braced at attention.

"Lieutenant Lawlor and Chief Cole, reporting as ordered, Sir," Jake sang out. A quick glance around the room revealed that in addition to team commander Porter, Jake's troop commander, Lieutenant Commander Forrest Clegg, was also in the room.

Something important is going down, Jake thought. Then he saw the topographical map pinned to the wall—Iran, the Gulf of Oman.

"At ease, gentlemen," Porter said. "Jake, Chief Cole, come and sit." The two men took the chairs he indicated. "Gentlemen, we may have just drawn a really important mission. The President hasn't given the final go-ahead yet, so there's not even a code name for it, but if we're going in—and the Secretary of the Navy, the Chief of Naval Operations, and Vice Admiral Williams (Commander, U.S. Special Operations

Command), think the chances are excellent that we will—then we have to be ready to move, and move quickly."

Porter then went on to explain the situation involving the six Americans being held in Iran, one of them the daughter of a sitting congressman. Jake had heard some of it already on the news, especially the part about how one of the detainees was the daughter of Congressman Longstreet, the VIP involved in the incident in Afghanistan where Hank Greenburg almost got his leg shot off.

When he had finished, Jake asked, "Do we have any intel at all on this Qajar prison, other than its general location, Sir?" Porter glanced over at Clegg, who rose to answer Jake's question for him.

"Not yet, Jake," Clegg began. "Just that it's located in, or at least around, this here city . . . (he pointed it out on the map) . . . Konarak, which is pretty much in the Iranian boondocks. Your job will be to put an infiltration team together and get yourselves ready to leave on the get-go. Rest assured that you and your infiltration team will have any additional info as soon as we do."

Jake was also attempted to ask "Why us?" But he knew better, and kept quiet. If Longstreet had anything to do with his team being selected for the mission or not, it was best not to ask. Instead, he walked over to the map on the wall, and Cole joined him.

Both Clegg and Porter remained silent while Jake and Cole examined the map. Konarak, they saw, was located in southeastern Iran, on the west bank of Chabahar Bay, a crenulated, omega-shaped, bay off the Gulf of Oman, east of the Strait of Hormuz and the Persian Gulf.

"From its location," Jake mused aloud, "the climate's got to be hot and hotter—not to mention damp."

Porter chuckled. "Exactly. But, at least this time of year, it's not the tourist season. Konarak's got a string of beaches along the gulf, and a really popular municipal beach on the bay. During the Summer, those beaches would have people on them at all hours—infiltration by water at this location would have been out of the question."

"We figured that you and the chief will need at least four other men, Jake," Clegg said. "So, for now, set up for a six-man infiltration and extraction."

Jake remained silent, thinking, *And that depends on exactly how big this Qajar prison is.*

Clegg continued. "And, as of now, until we know *if* we're going, and exactly *where* we're going, plan to infiltrate by submarine, and extract, with the six civilians, by helicopter."

"Why not just go in and out by chopper, Sir?" inquired Cole. "It would be a lot quicker. And what if there *are* some people on the beaches?"

"Good questions," Clegg said. "A few reasons. If there *are* people on the beaches, they are more likely to notice, and be alarmed by, a chopper flying in overhead, especially at night. But with a boat landing team, we can assume you would be far quieter, and certainly less noticeable (he paused for effect) . . . *especially* after dark. Then too, even after we pin down the prison's exact location, it's doubtful we'll know exactly where inside the prison the prisoners are being held."

Both men listened intently.

Clegg went on. "So you may well be spending more time finding them than the maximum half-hour typically allotted for a helicopter on site. Further, if this prison is inside, or close to, this city, then it's also just as well that we don't announce your arrival to the whole populace with a noisy helicopter (another pregnant pause) . . . and this area just west of Konarak (Clegg pointed to a complex of buildings and a small airfield on the map) is a major Iranian Naval Air Base, the place where they launch their unmanned aerial vehicles."

Jake nodded in acknowledgment.

"Then there's the Konarak Military Air Base just ten klicks north of the city," Clegg said, "that also doubles as a civilian airport. There's a squadron of MIG-23s that fly out of there, and our intel says they are on continuous alert—ready to scramble on short notice. And, oh yes, see this marina built out into Chabahar Bay, just east of the city?"

"Yessir," Jake said.

"Well," Clegg continued, "that's the home port for the city's fishing fleet—fishing and tourism being the town's major industries—but it's also home port for four of the Iranian Navy's patrol boats. And each of them is equipped with AA guns. And so, gentlemen, in summary, the stealthier the infiltration, the better. Even for the extraction, if we are to use helicopters at all, the operation must be in and out, just stopping long enough to embark you and the civilians, and then get all of you the hell out of Dodge."

"Understood, Sir," Jake replied. "One thing, though. I don't know if anyone on the team speaks any Farsi. Pashto, maybe, but no Farsi."

"Turns out it wouldn't make much difference, even if they did," Porter chimed in. "While whoever is guarding the prison, most likely Iranian regulars, probably speak Farsi, the natives in this area speak Balochi—whatever in blazes language *that* is." He paused, eyeing Lawlor and Cole. "And that's all we have for now. Now make ready to haul ass on short notice."

Clegg spoke again. "One more thing before you go, gentlemen," he said, as Jake and Cole made ready to leave.

"There will be no plywood mock-ups or team rehearsals on this operation. We will not have the time for the usual drill. Admiral Williams says the president wants these people *out*, like yesterday. That means that once we get the word, we move fast, and we move with whatever we know as soon as we know it."

Clegg looked from Jake to Cole, letting what he had just said sink in. "More later," he finished. "Dismissed."

One thing Clegg and Porter hadn't told Jake and Cole was that the president, at the urging of Mississippi Representative Longstreet, had *strongly* requested that the mission be given not just to a SEAL team, but to a SEAL team led by Lt. Jake Lawlor.

* * * * *

Later, on their way back to the SEAL compound, Jake asked Cole, "Well, so what do you think, Billy?"

"I think that pulling the Congressman's ass out of the fire in Kandahar is the reason we got this gig. Not sure we did ourselves any favors. Maybe we should have let him get wounded just a little bit or something." He was grinning when he added that, and Jake knew he wasn't serious.

"They sure as hell aren't giving us much information to go on," Jake opined.

"True that," Cole said. "And I think that whoever ordered this operation in the first place with practically no intel whatever is a nut case"

Jake chuckled. "No, Billy, I mean it. Tell me how you *really* feel."

"Not funny, Jake. How can they possibly expect us to go in and get these people out alive, when we don't know anything besides the name and location of the city where they're being held?" Cole then lowered the timbre of his voice in a poor imitation of Lt. Cdr. Clegg. "And, oh yes, by the way," he said, "the city is surrounded by unfriendly military facilities, and then, there's even the possibility of civilians being all over our landing site. And, oh yeah, since we don't know crap about the place we're sending you to, there's no point in practicing for the operation in advance." Then, in his normal voice, he said, "Smacks of exactly the way our glorious Commander-in-Chief has been running things from the get-go." Cole made no attempt to hide his extreme dislike of the sitting president.

"Ours is but to do and die, Billy."

"*Still* not funny."

Jake changed the subject, asking Cole in a serious tone: "How do you do it, Billy?"

"Do what? Mock command? That's what we white hats do!"

"No, not that. How do you deploy to a shit storm like Afghanistan, go out on missions like this one, knowing that you could easily never come back, and still be married and raise a family?"

Cole chuckled. "Getting to you, is she?"

"What?"

"Julie. She's getting to you."

"What . . . no. Well, maybe, just a little. Enough to think I wouldn't expect her to put up with what we do: always wondering when the next goodbye will be the last."

"Bullshit, Jake. And you know it. Married or not, you just do your job and don't worry about it. Of course, it takes a spectacular breed of woman—like my Emma. But she knew exactly what she was signing up for when she married me. And, if nothing else, she and my kids give me an excellent

73

reason to pay attention to my shit and not make stupid mistakes!"

Jake said nothing in reply. After a bit, Cole continued:

"Maybe Julie is that kind of woman, maybe not. But you'll never know unless you just come out and ask her."

Again, Jake remained silent. But, then, they had already reached the SEAL compound.

11

The Colonel

Konarak

Colonel Farshid Shir-Del Salehrad, Ministry of Intelligence of the Islamic Republic of Iran (SAVAK) was a pleasant-looking man of average height and build, a man who in no way looked threatening — unless, of course, he wanted to. His liquid onyx eyes, neat moustache, and closely trimmed beard gave him an air of elegance — an appearance in stark contrast to the unkempt, grizzle-bearded look of his Islamic-fanatic youth. Now the elegant, polished Salehrad, less religious, but no less a fanatic, served as a designated intelligence specialist. As such, he had studied the methods used by the Chinese to "brainwash" their American prisoners in the 1950-53 Korean War, as well as the methods used by the Soviet NKVD in the Lubianka prison to obtain signed bogus confessions. He had been tasked to use these same methods to break the six American detainees.

And while it should have been relatively easy to break six naïve Americans, the powers above him had not made the job at all easy. First, they had given him an almost impossible deadline: He had just six weeks to make them publically confess to their crimes. Second, he had to perform his magic under the worst conditions.

Instead of interrogating the prisoners in Teheran, where the facilities available to him were ideal, he was forced to do the job in God-forsaken Konarak, in a criminally inadequate facility. And — oh yes — he was to use drugs only as a last resort. The powers above felt that confessions delivered by automatons "under the influence" would be unconvincing on camera. With that observation, at least, the colonel was in agreement.

Qajar prison was at least two hundred years old, built by a long-dead shah, first as a provincial headquarters, and later converted to a prison to hold Baloch insurgents. As such, it featured two large iron cages, set in a single, large, underground holding cell. In each cage, the shah's army would house more than fifty Baloch prisoners. (Apparently those who could not be so accommodated were simply shot.) Also underground were two interrogation rooms, and a well-equipped interrogation (torture) chamber.

On the ground-level floor of the prison were two small private offices, a large storage room, and a cooking and dining facility for the prison staff. An upper floor served as a barracks for the prison staff, with a separate, private, bedroom for the camp superintendent (which Salehrad eschewed. When he did sleep, he preferred sleeping in the top-floor suite of a nearby hotel in town). An outside, high-walled courtyard off the ground floor featured a gang shower, a small storage shed, a newly-installed generator, and gang toilets.

The complex received water from the city system, which was fairly reliable, and it was connected to the city electric grid, which was not. Hence the generator. The bright lights that were lit day and night above the prisoner cages must never be allowed to go out.

Salehrad would have preferred that each prisoner be kept in solitary confinement, but the best he could do was separate the men from the women visually with a hastily-built, cement block wall. The colonel had also arranged for loud *Bakhsi* music to be piped into the holding cell, but the necessary equipment had not yet arrived from Teheran.

Still, Salehrad had been pleased with the progress thus far. His ministry staff had performed well, carrying out his orders without question. Then he received the news that one of the women, Clare Tindal, was the daughter of a U.S. congressman. And so it was that he now concentrated his efforts on her. And Clare Tindal was almost ready to break. He was sure that once one of the group broke, the others, like dominoes, would soon follow. All he had to do was keep up the pressure.

Salehrad had learned early on that to convince a subject that they had actually committed the crime for which they were being charged, he *himself* had to believe they had done it. Reality meant nothing. After all, if he could not *himself* suspend reality, neither could the subject. They must come to accept and *believe* they had done the crime, just as much as *he* believed. Reality was beside the point. Wearing down the subject physically and mentally were just a means to an end — to teach the subject to accept and to *believe*.

He sat in the interrogation room, smoking one of the long, thin, Turkish cigarettes he favored, as Clare Tindal was marched into the room. Her fellow prisoner, Adele Crowley, he knew, was soon to enjoy the tender attentions of his men in the large chamber down the hall. He watched as Clare's cuffs were removed, and smiled at her after the hood was removed from her head. The woman was filthy, disheveled, bruised, and flea-bitten. And she stank. Still, the colonel managed a smile. He smiled as if he were genuinely delighted to see her, and because he had been able to convince himself that he actually was.

"Please, Clare, sit . . . Here, have some water." Clare sat quickly, grabbing and greedily draining the contents of the plastic bottle.

"Easy, Clare, Easy. I would not want you to choke," Salehrad said, with his perfect English and clipped British public-school accent. Clare glanced sideways at the man, reluctant to meet his pellucid black eyes. He wore the usual impeccable uniform, with its leather-belted, forest green jacket, three gold pips on black epaulets. "Are you getting enough to eat?" he asked, apparent genuine concern dripping from his mouth.

"No," she said. "You know I am not. None of us are."

"Ah, Clare, but you could, you know. You *all* could." Muffled by distance and sound-proofing in the interrogation room, there was nonetheless a sudden scream heard from down the hall. Clare shivered and tried to fold her body up onto itself, hunching her shoulders and clutching her sides.

"You could be clean, well-fed, well-treated. You could sleep in a real bed again, with clean sheets," the colonel continued, as if the scream had been entirely in Clare's imagination. "And all the *bad* things would stop. All you have to do is cooperate. I'm really here just to help you. You know, it *pains* me to see you hurt. But I cannot stop others from hurting you unless you admit to the truth. It is you who gives us no choice in the matter. But you, Clare, *you* have a choice. You and all of your friends do. You *all* have a choice. All you have to do is tell me the truth, and all of this will be over. Just admit to what we both know to be true, that you are the daughter of a sitting U.S. congressman..."

Clare Tindal's eyes widened. *He knew. They had found her out. They had broken John. Her husband must have told them.*

Salehrad continued as if he hadn't observed her reaction "And admit that you and your companions are spies for the United States, and in a few days later you will be on a plane to Paris. That, I can do. That I can promise. But, first, you must cooperate, and tell me the truth."

"Paris?" she said.

And he knew that soon she would be his.

12

Moses

East Beach, Virginia

Only married officers get a housing allowance. Still, Jake could have lived on the base in the Bachelor Officer's Quarters (BOQ) for free. But he opted, instead, to rent a small apartment with an ocean view in East Beach, not far from the base. The place was sparsely furnished, but had everything Jake needed, including a 54-inch LED TV (basic cable came with the rent), and a fridge adequately stocked with Budweiser. And he could jog on the beach most mornings.

His only roommate was a sleek, solid-black tomcat he had named Moses. He really didn't want to keep an animal, much less a cat—he was more of a dog person—but Moses had suckered him into adopting him. Not that he had put up much of a fight.

Nine months earlier, and, before his Afghanistan tour, Jake had just returned from the base. He had parked his Jeep Wrangler, and was walking up the shrubbery-lined path leading to the entrance to his building when he heard a pathetic squeal coming from the foliage. He investigated, and its source was a tiny black kitten with bright yellow eyes, yowling for all it was worth. Jake picked him up, and the little thing fit easily in the palm of his hand. The kitten immediately stopped mewling, and began to purr. Jake could hardly believe that such a little thing could purr so loudly. So, of course, he took him up to his apartment.

"Whatcha got there?" asked Julie, his then recently acquired next door neighbor, who was hauling a laundry-basket full of folded clothes up from the basement. Jake had been attracted to her from the moment he first saw her. Jet black hair, and doe-brown eyes that he could drown in.

"Kitten," Jake said, holding it out to show her.

"Oh, how cute! Where'd you find it?"

"In the bushes outside. Poor thing must have been abandoned."

"You gonna keep it?"

"Don't know how I can. I'm not home all that much, and I'm scheduled to deploy next month. I'll be gone for six months. I'll be subletting my apartment, so I can't keep him here, even if I could find somebody else willing to look after him, and I can *hardly* take a kitten to Afghanistan."

"I get it," she said, "but please don't take him to the pound! Look, while you're not here, I could always take care of him for you. I'm pretty much tied down to my job, and I hardly ever go anywhere. Please keep him! I can keep him in my apartment while you're gone, and I'll take care of him for you!"

"What you mean is that *you* want to keep him. And that's okay. You've got yourself a kitten!" Extending his arm, he held the kitten out to her.

Julie thought fast. Here was a chance to set up a connection between her handsome neighbor and herself. The truth was, that the attraction between them was mutual, even if neither one had yet let on. "Oh no, I couldn't do that. *You* found him. He's yours. I just said I'll watch him for you while you're gone. Then, when you come back, he'll still be yours."

Jake wasn't sure what the difference was, or that it even made any sense that Julie was unwilling to claim the kitten as her own. After all, she'd be watching it fulltime for the next six months, anyway—but he didn't argue. The little bugger was awfully cute after all, and he really didn't want to take it to the pound, either. "Well, okay Jules, as long as you'll watch him for me while I'm gone. You're sure, now —"

"I'm sure! He's yours, and I'll just be watching him for you. Whatcha gonna call him?"

"Hadn't thought about it." He paused. "Guess, if it's a male, and I'm keeping him, I'll call him Moses, 'cause I found him in the bulrushes."

Julie laughed. "Moses, eh? That's perfect."

A visit to the vet, and the kitten was identified as definitely male. Moses was then relieved of his fleas and any other parasites. He was also relieved of his testicles. The vet said that Moses was about six weeks old.

And that was nine months ago.

Now, Jake had to admit that he had, over the past nine months, thought about both Moses and Julie quite often. Especially Julie. As much as he wanted to pursue a relationship with his beautiful neighbor, he held back: after all, how could he ask *any* woman to share his dangerous life?

He knocked on his neighbor's door. "Jules, you home?"

"Minute, Jake," a disembodied voice from behind the door answered.

About a minute later, the door opened, and Julie O'Leary appeared in the doorway, holding two opened bottles of

Budweiser. She looked good, even in jeans and a tee shirt. She handed one of the bottles to Jake. "What do you need?" she asked. "You never knock at my door unless you need *something*." She may well have been serious, but she said it with a broad smile.

Taking the proffered beer, Jake smiled back. Julie could easily be, he knew, just like another little sister — very much like the two others he grew up with. That was, of course, if he could ever be satisfied with just a brother-sister relationship.

Except for her coloring, Julie might even be his sisters' triplet. Despite the O'Leary name, Julie was mostly Italian-American. Her mother's parents were Italian-born, and her dad was Italian-American on his mother's side. And Jake couldn't help but also notice that Julie was equally as pretty, even if in a different way, as either of his sisters. She had an oval face, raven-colored hair, a thin, straight, nose, and brown, brown eyes, like melted dark chocolate. Her full lips could break into a dazzling smile at the slightest urging. She also had a figure most women would sell their souls for. His sisters, on the other hand, were both so obviously Irish-American — fair skin and auburn hair — it was pathetic. Yes, Julie could be just like another little sister. But, if Jake would only admit it to himself, in his increasingly frequent reveries, Julie wouldn't behave anything like a sister to him.

But getting back to the reason for his visit: "Jules, I may be deploying again on short notice. Be gone for possibly a week, maybe longer. I really don't know. I may not even get a chance to text you before I go, so if I don't come home tomorrow, can you check on Moses for me?"

"Sure," she said. "Happy to." She took a sip of her beer.

"Thanks, Jules," he said, smiling. "You're an absolute angel."

And Jules thought, *And you're an absolute idiot. When are you gonna make your move, Jake Lawlor?* But she smiled back at him just the same. "Your buddy Bill going with?" she asked.

"Sure, Billy Cole's my right hand." She knew Cole only because Bill and Emma Cole had demanded he take a date to their "Welcome Back" cookout when the platoon came back from Afghanistan. Jake never considered asking anyone but Julie, but wasn't sure about the best way to broach the subject to her. So, instead, he just asked her "to hang with him," at the cookout and she'd agreed.

Julie had made a real hit with the Coles, and their little three-year-old girl, Kelly, kept asking Jake, "You gonna marry her?" Since then, every now and again, Cole kept asking him how Julie was.

"Well, say 'Hi,' " she said.

"I will. And Jules . . ."

"Yes?"

"Thank you for looking after Moses. I really appreciate it."

"My pleasure," she said. "Moses and I are best buds."

"You are," he agreed. "You know, I really think he probably loves you more than he loves me."

Well, at least that's one of you, Julie thought, and just smiled. *Men are really such idiots. Some Navy men, in particular, it seems.*

13

Konarak City

Konarak

Hamid Alinejad spent a fairly unpleasant night in his suite. The weather outside had cooled considerably from the heat of the daytime, and so he opened the window to catch the breeze blowing in from the gulf. After he opened the window, however, he thought better of it. The night air was indeed cooler, but it was also oppressively damp. Shutting the window, he instead turned on the air conditioner.

Sometime during the night, however, the power went off, and he awoke hot and sweaty. A glance out the window that looked out over the city told him that there was nothing wrong with the air conditioner. The unrelenting darkness outside was evidence enough that the power was out throughout Konarak. After he threw off the thin sheet blanket that had covered him, he was a bit cooler, but, somehow, the outside damp had managed to infiltrate the suite. Eventually, he fell back asleep. But when the power did come back on, so did the air conditioner, and he again awoke, this time cold and clammy.

* * * * *

In Qajar prison, the power also went off. Automatically and almost immediately, the generator in the outside courtyard fired up, and restored the flow of electricity to the building. The off-duty guards in the upper room slept through the entire incident. In the basement, the bright lights illuminating the cages flickered only briefly. As with the guards, the physically and emotionally exhausted, bruised, and abused prisoners sleeping fitfully on the concrete floor, never noticed.

* * * * *

In the third-floor suite of the hotel in town, Colonel Salehrad slept on top of the bed in his underwear, the air conditioner shut off, the widows of the suite open to the night air and the wet gulf breeze. Like the Qajar sleepers, the loss of power in the town didn't affect him in the least.

* * * * *

At 6:30 in the morning, Hamid Alinejad, dressed casually in cotton khaki slacks and a solid blue polo shirt with long sleeves, went down to the hotel dining room for breakfast. Already seated across the room was a man in green uniform jacket and black trousers. The uniform identified him as SAVAK. The man had slicked-back, black hair, a neat beard, and otherwise rather pleasant features. When he glanced briefly over at Hamid, however, he could see that the colonel's piercing black eyes could, if they so intended, strike terror into anyone who had merited the man's disfavor. This, Hamid correctly surmised, was Colonel Farshid Salehrad. Hamid nodded to the colonel. The colonel nodded back, acknowledging Hamid's presence, and then turned again to his breakfast.

Hamid noted that the colonel was enjoying a full, English-style breakfast. He correctly guessed that Salehrad had probably spent at least a few of his formative years in England. He, instead, contented himself with more typical Iranian fare, some fig jam spread on Iranian thin bread, nuts, cheese, and black tea.

The colonel finished breakfast and strode purposefully out of the dining room. Hamid followed not long afterward, but in the lobby, stopped to ask the desk clerk where he might rent a bicycle. The clerk, a different man from the one who had rented the suite to Hamid, told him that the hotel kept some bicycles for the use of their guests, and that he would be happy to get him one. The clerk called out in a language Hamid didn't recognize, and an elderly man in a rumpled uniform suddenly appeared at the desk, apparently arriving out of thin air. The clerk spoke some instructions to the man in the same unintelligible language. The man left, and the clerk handed Hamid a map of the city, telling him that a bicycle would be waiting for him outside the building in a few minutes.

Hamid strode outside the hotel. Out on the street, he surveyed the 7:00 AM activity. The colonel's Mercedes, he noted, was gone from the curb. His own Boxster was still where he had parked it, apparently having survived the night unmolested. He expected to find street traffic rather thin at this hour, but was surprised at its being fairly heavy. There were cars of every style, make, and vintage: Renaults, Toyotas, Volkswagens, and even a few European-manufactured Fords. But mostly there were bicycles and mopeds.

When Hamid turned, the old man from the hotel was there, holding out a bicycle. It was a black street bike, with hand brakes, a three-speed gearshift, and skinny tires. He thanked him, mounted the bike, and, referring to the map of the city the clerk had given him, he located both the location of his drop box, and the road leading to the marina.

Conveniently, the drop box would be on the way. The drop box was exactly as it had been described: a public bench set against a blank east wall on the corner of Maymunah Street and Bayshore Drive. As he pedaled by, he noted there was no chalk mark on the wall above the bench. There would be no hidden thumb drive with information or instructions. Nothing for him today.

The marina was at the end of a long dock, a plank roadway really, that extended out three kilometers into the bay. The plank roadway extended from Bayshore and crossed the beach at the opposite corner of the town from the hotel. *So much for the hotel's being convenient to the marina,* Alinejad thought, and resolved to say a few words to the desk clerk who had misinformed him.

Upon reaching the marina itself, Hamid surveyed the scene. Most of the boat slips were empty, the fishing fleet having left the night before, and probably just now on its way back into the bay. At the very end of the pier there were four Iranian Navy patrol boats tied up perpendicular to the dock, their crews nowhere in evidence. He finally spied what he was looking for: a half-dozen boats closer in, with signs on the dock in both Persian script and English, saying: "Sport Fishing."

Hamid parked his bicycle and headed toward the nearest of the sport-fishing dhows. Nobody was aboard. He went further down the dock, and finally found one of the boats with a man aboard, hosing down the deck. On the bow was the name "*Roya*," written in Persian script, and, written again beneath the script, in English. The dhow was gaily painted in bright blues, pinks, and reds. "Is the *Roya* for hire?" he asked the man in Farsi, who only then noticed him, eying him suspiciously.

"It is off-season," the man said, replying in the same language. He was of indeterminate age, sun-wrinkled, with a bulbous nose and rheumy brown eyes. He wore a faded baseball cap, once black, now mostly gray, with an American sports team logo on it: a snorting bull. A torn tee shirt and ancient, faded blue jeans worn over bare feet completed the ensemble.

"True," Hamid answered, "But the fish do not know it is off-season."

The man aboard the boat was not amused. "I can take you out, if you want," he said, "but it is off-season. There is no one to come out with you."

"But you *will* take me out?"

"If you have the fare. You are by yourself. Normally, three or four men would split the cost. What currency will you be using?"

"Euros." Hamid answered, and the man smiled broadly, displaying yellow, broken teeth. "How much?" Hamid asked.

The man quoted an outrageously high price, and the two men haggled from there. Eventually, after a few minutes, they agreed on a much more reasonable price, although Hamid was still certain that he was paying too much. Then the man held out his hand and Hamid paid him the agreed-upon amount.

"Wait here," the man told Hamid. "I will go and get some ice, bait, and something for lunch. I will be back in fifteen minutes. If anyone comes looking for me, tell them I will be right back."

"Okay. And who exactly will they be looking for?"

"Amir," he said. "I am called Amir." Then he padded off the boat and walked to a metallic-blue moped parked on the dock, started the machine, and tore off down the plank road back toward town.

Fifteen minutes passed, then twenty. After twenty-five minutes, Hamid wondered if he would see Amir again that day. Or ever. Then he heard the high-pitched whine of the moped and spied Amir coming back down the plank road. When the moped reached the boat, Hamid was amazed at how much Amir was able to transport on the tiny machine: four large bags of ice, a 20-litre bucket of bait, and a paper sack, which, he assumed, held their lunch.

When all was loaded aboard the *Roya*, and with Hamid aboard, Amir backed the dhow expertly off the dock, and headed out into the bay.

14

Aboard the *Roya*

Gulf of Oman

On the trip out into the gulf, the *Roya* passed the fishing fleet coming in toward the marina.

The *Roya* was sturdy enough, Hamid reckoned, broad-beamed and about twelve or thirteen meters long. The bay, at least, had been dead calm, and he hoped the gulf would be no different. He had not been out in a boat for some time, but he knew he was not a good sailor. He was gratified to find the gulf was every bit as calm as the bay. Blue, blue water rippled only by a gentle breeze. The sky a deep blue with not a cloud in sight.

"What will we be fishing for?" he asked Amir.

"Depends on what Allah sends us," Amir answered. "The sailfish run year-round, as do tuna and trevally, but they are best beginning next month through May. When we get to a good place, I will put out five trawling lines. If you sit in one of the swivel chairs on the stern, when we get a hit, I will hand you the line, and you can bring the catch into the boat. If we hook a sailfish, will you want to keep it as a trophy?"

"No, I do not think so."

"Very well. That is good. Then just bring it to the boat, and I will snap the line and release the hook. Then the fish will live to fight another day."

About a half-hour later, the *Roya* must have gotten to "a good place" because Amir baited the huge hooks on five trawling lines, and began running alternatively west and then east in straight lines, which Hamid guessed were about six or seven kilometers long.

The day was pleasant enough, although hot, with a brilliant sun rising in that cloudless, azure sky — the heat tempered only by that lazy breeze. Amir produced a broad-brimmed, floppy hat and gave it to Alinejad saying, "Here, put this on. You can burn up out here."

"What about you?" Hamid asked. "Will you not burn up as well?"

Amir chuckled. "I burnt up a long time ago. Back when the shah was still running the country."

The *Roya* went back and forth, for, what seemed to Hamid, several hours. The sun had just passed its zenith, and he was chewing on a lamb sandwich, made with a flatbread and dripping *tzatziki*, when, suddenly, one of the rods started running line, the reel spinning. Amir grabbed the rod and set the reel, jerking back the line to set the hook.

Just then, a beautiful sailfish, all gorgeous iridescent blue and silver, with its sail fin unfurled, jumped out of the water well off the dhow's port quarter. Hamid barely had a chance to admire the sight before Amir handed him the rod. In grabbing for it, he dropped the forgotten sandwich.

"Play him," Amir directed. "Reel in and pull back on the rod. The reel is set to give line whenever he decides to start running. Let him run, and when he stops, start reeling him in again." Amir then reeled in the other four lines, lest they foul the line in play.

Hamid fought the fish for a good three hours, and each time he thought he had tired the fish out, and began reeling him in, the beast would once again jump out of the water, shaking its spiked snout in an effort to lose the hook, and then fall back into the water, again taking line. When he finally brought the magnificent animal up to the boat, he was not sure which of them was more exhausted. Amir looked over the stern into the water. The fish, tired out now, was on its side, floating just beneath the surface.

"A truly beautiful animal," Amir allowed. "I would guess thirty, maybe thirty-five kilos, and at least two hundred and sixty centimeters. Magnificent."

Hamid peered over the stern, savoring his catch.

"Sure you do not want to keep him?" Amir asked. "People *do* eat them."

"No one will eat him," Hamid replied, "not today at least. Let him go."

Amir gave Hamid an approving look, gave the line a sharp jerk, and released the hook. The sailfish rolled slowly over and disappeared into the deep.

"I am beat. I am done for the day," Hamid told Amir. "I am ready to head in."

"You sure?" Amir asked. "It is just half-past three o'clock. We have several hours left until dusk."

"I am sure," he answered.

On the way in, Hamid asked Amir, "So, you remember life under the shah?"

"Of course I do. I may have been just a boy when the British and the Soviets invaded the country and deposed Reza

93

Shah, but I remember the rule of his eldest son, Emperor Mohammad Reza Shah very well."

"Ah," Hamid said, "and I was still a twinkle in the eye of my father when *he* was deposed. I have never known anything other than the Islamic Republic." (Hamid carefully noted Amir's expression when he mentioned the Republic. If he had read his expression correctly, Amir was apparently not at all sympathetic to the current regime.)

Back at the marina, Hamid made arrangements with Amir to go out again the next morning. He had rested up somewhat while the *Roya* had motored back from the gulf, and though he no longer felt exhausted, his arms and shoulders still ached. In reflecting back on the day, however, recalling his struggle with that beautiful sailfish, he decided he never before had as much fun with his clothes on.

Hamid then got back on the bicycle and rode back into the city. It was still not yet five o'clock, and he had some work to do before the day was over.

There was still no chalk mark on the wall behind the public bench.

He then played at being a tourist, riding the bicycle throughout the town, actually doing a reconnaissance—in depth. Konarak was, he knew (because Google had said so), a city of about 45,000 regular inhabitants, which swelled to twice that number in the summer months. And it appeared that, with the pleasant weather (despite the heat), at least half of the regular population was out and about that afternoon.

In Konarak, Hamid felt alienated, just as he had when he first experienced Teheran, surrounded by Farsi speakers. The spoken language was so different from that in Israel, where the sound of Hebrew was so familiar and so comfortable. But in Teheran, at least, he had studied and understood Farsi. He was fluent in it, and had even trained himself to think in that language. But here, in Konarak, the *lingua franca* was Balosh, a tongue both foreign and unintelligible, so here he felt completely alienated. Were it not for the occasional passersby conversing in Farsi, he might have thought he had left Iran altogether.

At one point in his wanderings, he came upon the roundabout with the monument in the center. He had driven around the monument the previous night. The monument was, he had to admit, one of the strangest he had ever seen. Mounted on a high pedestal was a brightly painted dhow, set at a downward angle to the roadway. *Most likely a monument to the town's principal means of employment – or perhaps placed here to amuse the tourists.*

This section of the city also contained an architectural monstrosity of a building (Soviet neo-realism, perhaps?), the home of the municipal government offices, including the local police.

Before one left the modern city and entered the old town, a large municipal square held the mosque. Four minarets surrounded a whitewashed, mushroom-cap dome. Moving on, inside the old town, he noted two municipal buildings, the library, and a municipal museum, that were obviously converted churches. At one time, certainly before the revolution, Christians (and perhaps Jews as well) had obviously been allowed to worship freely in Konarak. No more.

When he knew there would only be about an hour or so of daylight left, he got on the main southbound road west of the town and headed toward the place in Konarak in which he was most interested: Qajar prison.

15

Know Thine Enemy

Washington, D.C.

The president had summoned the secretary of defense, his national security advisor, and the director of the CIA to the Oval Office. The secretary of state was conspicuous by his absence. Today the president wore a blue, pinstriped business suit and a bright red tie. When he stormed into the room, the three stood up and greeted him in unison: "Mr. President."

"Marine One is waiting," he said, "so we'll just skip the pleasantries. Look, I'm tired of Harry Fielding's assurances that he can get our people out of Iran with a long-distance circle jerk. I'm letting him keep trying, but that road's going nowhere. It's a dead end . . .

"So, look, Gordy," he continued, "I'm giving you the go ahead. Send those SEALs in there—the team I asked for—and get those people out. Charlie and Helen, give Gordy and his people everything you've got, and help him in any way you can. Everybody got it?"

Three heads nodded simultaneously.

"Great. Now I've got to attend some silly-ass ceremony in Maryland," he said, and stormed out of the room. None of them had said a single word beyond their greeting.

"The SEAL team's been on alert since yesterday," Gordon Jones told the others, "but I can't just send them to Iran without more intel. You guys have gotten us some good stuff from the Israelis already, but we need more. Crap, we don't even have an exact location of the place they're being held . . ."

"We'll get right on it, Gordy," Siebert assured him, "and anything we find out we'll pass on to you immediately. Meanwhile, why don't you get the Air Force to get one of those new stealth surveillance drones up over Konarak, ASAP. You know, one of those new birds that can spot a dime on the ground from sixty thousand feet?"

"Right," Jones said, and hurried out. "As if there really was such a thing." He knew the new drones were good, all right, but he didn't think they were that good.

16

Yasmina and Taraneh

Konarak

Having left the town center and heading the bicycle south along the main road, Hamid carefully observed and memorized as he proceeded, noting every landmark, the surrounding bleak countryside, every bend in the road. Compared to the traffic in town, there were very few passing cars here. It was still as hot, but somehow it didn't seem as hot as it had in Teheran this time of year. *Must be the open space and a sea breeze,* he thought. *Less concrete and asphalt to trap and hold the heat.*

He pedaled the bicycle lazily, not just because of the heat, but also to maintain his cover as a tourist, just taking in the sights.

Hamid had just left the southeast edges of town behind him, when he spied what had to be Qajar prison, about 150 meters or so off the main road. The building, made entirely of mold-blackened concrete, faced south, away from him, onto a dirt road that sat perpendicular to the main road. First in view was a walled-in courtyard of some sort, in the rear of the building, topped with silver concertina wire. The concrete courtyard walls were, he estimated, at least four meters high, or about one-half the height of the two-story building itself. There was no apparent activity—no people, no noise. As he passed the building, he noted that the colonel's Mercedes was parked out front.

Hamid stayed on the main road and continued pedaling south. Traffic was still very light, just two or three cars in the past half hour or so.

He pedaled on for about another 500 meters. Then the roadway dipped sharply down for what looked like another 100 meters, before it flattened out and continued south. Not thrilled with the idea of continuing onward, and then having to pedal back up the steep hill, Hamid stopped there, laying down the bike. He walked about, surveying the landscape. Not far off in the distance he could see the blue water of the Gulf of Oman. He noted the roadway that branched off in both directions from the main road and paralleled the shoreline. Both the roadway and the beach below were deserted. He also saw the reason for the sharp dip in the main road: a cliff at least fifteen meters high that also paralleled the shoreline, well up from, and well off, the beach. The cliff stretched out in both directions, east and west, as far as he could see.

If the Americans are coming in from the sea, Hamid thought, *they had best travel the roadway. I would hate to have to scale that cliff. They could, of course, come in by the Bay. No cliffs there. But then they would have to go through town to reach the prison.*

He mounted the bicycle and headed back north. As he again approached the prison, he noted that the front of the building had a single entrance, and that the colonel's car was still there, parked just to the right of the door. There was no door on the side of the building facing the main road, but there could possibly be one on the other end, away from the main road, or perhaps even another, off the courtyard, on that side.

There was no way he could tell without going around to the other side of the building and looking. He wondered if he should chance riding down the dirt road past the prison, but then thought better of it. Even though a curious tourist might investigate the interesting building from the side road, it would be well not to draw any undue attention to himself, lest he should be noticed by anyone inside the building.

There were windows along the upper floor, four in front, and one on the west end. There were also windows on either side of the doorway on the first floor, and another on the end. He remembered that there were no windows at the rear of the place. The roof was flat, and it appeared that it was edged with at least a short wall, as the top of the building was crenellated, giving the whole place a sense of foreboding, as though it were some sort of castle, or, more appropriately, a fort.

He continued pedaling north, resolved to go far enough to be out of sight of the prison, wait until after dark, and then return for additional reconnaissance. It was closing in on seven o'clock as he lay down the bike a ways off the roadway, and settled in to wait.

He had not waited long before it became as dark as it was going to get. Hamid was concerned that the night was crystal clear, and with the quarter-moon high in the still cloudless sky, the visibility was excellent. Nonetheless, he had picked up the bike with every intention of heading back to Qajar prison for that additional recon, when he heard some talking and giggling coming up from the roadway. *Could very well be the two women that cook and clean the place,* he thought, and rode out to meet them, if, indeed, it was them. He positioned his bike on the roadway, and pedaled very slowly north, slow enough for the two women to overtake him (again, if it *was* them).

Sure enough, two bicycles approached from the south, and began to pull past him. The talking and giggling had ceased, and they passed him warily. Hamid could see them well enough to establish that they were modestly dressed, and wore head scarves.

Religious, he thought, and used the religious form of greeting. *"Salaam alaikum* [peace be with you]."

"Alaikum salaam," was the automatic response [and with you, peace]. Hamid quickened his pace, and rode up beside them.

"Good evening, ladies," he said, in Farsi, hoping for a more informal response.

"Good evening," one of them responded in Farsi. Immediately the other woman, the one farthest from him, spoke sharply to the responder, in *Balochi.* Hamid, of course, did not understand her, but by now, at least, could recognize the sound and rhythm of the local patois, and identified it as such. The responder snapped back just as sharply in kind, and then said sweetly, in Farsi, "How are you?" to Hamid.

"I am fine," he said. "I am called Hamid. Your friend appears not to be too friendly."

"Taraneh is very religious, and *very* married. She does not approve of speaking to any man who has not been formally introduced by a close relative. I am Yasmina, Hamid."

"Hello, Yasmina. Your Farsi is perfect. Where did you learn to speak the language so well?"

"My father is a fishmonger, and my family runs a small fish store. I normally work there, and we sell to the tourists in the summer. Since they mostly speak Farsi, I just naturally picked up the language."

"I see," Hamid said. "You said your friend Taraneh is very religious. And you, Yasmina, you are not of like mind? I can see you wear the *dastmaal* [head scarf]."

"She is not really my friend. And the *dastmaal*, and the rest of the frumpy clothing, is for the job," she said. "The man who interviewed us and hired us for this work insisted we be dressed and behave modestly."

Hamid feigned alarm. "But surely you do that all the time!" he said.

"I do!" she protested. "Well, behave, anyway. But I *hate* these frumpy clothes."

"But you look lovely in them," Hamid said, flattering her.

"It is dark," Yasmina countered. "You can hardly see me at all, and I can only look frumpy with no make-up and in these frumpy clothes."

There followed another exchange in *Balochi* between Yasmina and Taraneh, the other woman scolding, Yasmina again responding angrily. They were coming up to the edge of the main town.

"I turn here," Yasmina said, as if the exchange with Taraneh had never taken place. She turned her bicycle to the right, and the other woman continued, in a huff, onward up the main road. Hamid turned as well, and kept pace with Yasmina.

"What brings you to our boring city?" Yasmina asked.

"The fishing," he responded, consistent with his cover story. "I am on vacation from my work in Teheran. I plan to stay at least through the week. Today, out in the gulf, I caught a sailfish."

"Really," she said, unimpressed.

"It was really fun," he protested. "I am going out again tomorrow. Would you like to come out with me—with me and my guide, of course."

"I could not, even if I wanted to," she said. "I have to work."

"How about on your day off?"

"I do not get a day off. Taraneh and I were hired for a guaranteed six weeks of work, but we had to agree to work every day, for the entire time, sunup to sundown. The pay is excellent, and neither Taraneh's husband nor my father would let us refuse the job."

"Sounds important," Hamid allowed.

"I do not see what is important about it. We just cook and clean for the eight slobs who are living there. The other one, the boss, does not stay there, although sometimes he takes meals with the others."

"And where is *there*?" Hamid asked.

"Qajar, the prison just outside of town. We were coming from there when you met us on the road."

"Ah, *that* place. I saw it as I rode my bike past. Looks like a fort or an old castle, and *very* ominous."

"Ominous is not the half of it. The working conditions are terrible, the men are filthy and uncouth, and there is something evil going on in the basement."

"Evil?"

"Evil. There are screams. I have complained to my father, but he will do nothing. He is afraid, and Taraneh and I are being paid too well. I cannot wait until this job is over."

They had ridden well into town at that point, and Hamid could see from the street lighting that Yasmina, while a large girl, and not more than twenty, was pretty, even if somewhat plain. She would, he imagined, end up married off to a local fisherman, and bear his children.

"Well," Yasmina said, "my home is just down the street." She stopped and sat astride her bike, as did Hamid on his.

"It is a shame you must work so much," Hamid said, "and that I will not be in town much longer. I really would like to get to know you better," He paused and then continued. "But you have to eat . . . can you at least come and have dinner with me?"

Her face brightened. "Yes! Stay here," she said. "I will be right back."

Hamid waited.

A half hour later, Yasmina reappeared, and had it not been for the familiar voice saying, "I am ready, let us go," he would have thought that this was an entirely different woman from the one who had ridden beside him on her bicycle. Yasmina was a large woman, but in a healthy, full-figured way, her body beautifully filling out the pretty blue dress she now wore. What had been a pretty, if somewhat plain, face, was now (thanks to some skillfully applied makeup) *very* pretty. She had large, dark brown—almost black—eyes, and long lashes, framed by shining black hair that cascaded over her shoulders, just covering her ample bosom. Hamid's reaction to this version of Yasmina—a plain, unattractive, girl, now transformed into an object of desire—was visceral.

"You look spectacular," he said, meaning it.

"Thank you! Not like that frumpy cleaning woman, eh?"

"Not at all! I'm surprised your parents let you out of the house looking so lovely!"

She laughed. "They didn't. They wouldn't. I snuck out. They think I'm safely tucked away in my bed for the night.

And after we say goodnight, I'll sneak back in. They will never know I've gone out!"

Hamid smiled. *This evening could get very interesting,* he thought, but he said: "The hotel has recommended a restaurant that they say . . ."

"Never mind that," she interrupted. "Anyplace that they recommend is an overpriced tourist trap. I know a place close by, run by a widow and her daughter. Small, quiet, excellent food, and very discreet. You will like it."

"Sounds great! Let us go there," he said.

The restaurant was every bit as good as Yasmina had promised. During dinner, Hamid pushed her for the details of her day job, and by the end of the meal, he had tucked away in his mind the layout of the prison, and the number and duties of the men living and working there. What she had been unable to tell him, was the layout of the basement level, since neither she nor Taraneh were ever allowed there. "Which is just as well," she had opined, "The screams coming up from there are frightening. People down there must be getting tortured. The two pigs that practically live down there, always come upstairs to eat covered with blood and filth. And they stink, the same stink that comes up from the stairwell. I don't want to even know what goes on down there, but I'm certain it's terrible!"

"It certainly does sound terrible," Hamid agreed.

"But I have told you everything about me, and you have told me next to nothing about yourself. I only know that you work in Teheran, and that you are here on vacation, and in Konarak for the fishing. What is your work?"

Hamid fed her his cover story, which was not actually untrue, since he had to have some sort of actual employment other than the main reason for his presence in the Islamic Republic: to spy on it for Israel.

"So," she said, "You're a businessman. Import, export, you connect buyers and sellers. Sounds interesting. Tell me, Hamid, would there be jobs available in Teheran for an enterprising woman such as myself?"

He knew where this was going. "Probably. Why do you ask?"

"Because I want you to take me back with you to Teheran! Please, Hamid, I am dying in this godforsaken city. I don't want to end up like poor Taraneh, married to some ugly, smelly, fisherman, with no purpose in life other than to produce even more ugly, smelly, little fishermen! Please, Hamid, take me back to Teheran with you!"

"But what about your parents? They would report you missing—the police would come after us—they would arrest me for kidnapping, and you would be taken right back here anyway!"

"No, they would not. And even if they do report me gone, I am of age. Even in Iran, my parents cannot force me to accept the old ways. Please, Hamid." And to encourage his cooperation, she reached under the table and stroked his leg. "I can be very grateful," she said, matter-of-fact.

Hamid knew to his core that this was a very bad idea. But he was only human—a *male* human—after all.

"Come with me back to the hotel," he said.

And Yasmina smiled a triumphant smile.

As the couple walked quickly back to the hotel, Yasmina cautioned that they would have to be quick about it, since there was no way she could spend the night. After all, she had to be back in her own bed before morning, and she *did* have to get up early for work.

Hamid, meanwhile, had convinced himself that the opportunity to glean more information from Yasmina was more than sufficient reason to bed her, and also to lie about intending to take her back with him to Teheran.

Hamid's only fear was that when they arrived at the hotel, they might run into the SAVAK colonel, and that the man might recognize his daytime prison cleaning woman (not that that was very likely in Yasmina's current incarnation). When they did arrive at the hotel, the colonel's Mercedes was parked out in front. Hamid hoped that Salehrad had followed his usual routine of a light dinner and early retirement. Thankfully, the colonel was nowhere in evidence, and no one seemed to notice, or to question, Hamid, when he snuck a giggling Yasmina up to his room.

When their tryst was over, and he had walked Yasmina home, Hamid had gleaned no more information from her then he had already learned at dinner. What he did discover was that Yasmina was skilled and enthusiastic in the bedroom, and that he had obviously not been her first lover. Somehow, it made his inevitably betraying her seem somewhat less caddish.

Before their parting kiss, and some affectionate groping, Yasmina agreed to meet him again for dinner the following evening, and they arranged a place and time to meet.

When Hamid returned to the hotel, he stayed there only long enough to record on a flash drive what he had learned from Yasmina about the prison layout, manning level, and daily routine. He then bicycled out to the drop box, placed the recording in a chink in the bench, and put a chalk mark on the wall. Then he crashed in his rumpled bed. Like Yasmina, he had also had to rise early. But to meet Amir and go out on the *Roya*.

The following morning, en route to the marina, Hamid noted that the chalk mark had been rubbed off. *The information on that thumb drive is probably already in Tel Aviv,* he thought, pleased.

17

Information is Currency

Washington, D.C.

With Cuthbert in tow, Siebert headed to her office in the White House basement.

As soon as they reached her office, Charles Cuthbert and Helen Siebert were once again on a secure line to Shlomo Rosenszweig in Tel Aviv.

"What have you got for us, Moe?" Siebert asked. "Our boss is chomping at the bit, and he's made up his mind to send the SEALs in even though we still don't know crap."

"Well," Rosenszweig began, "I know a lot more now than I knew even an hour ago. We have placed an agent on the ground in Konarak and this is what we found out. This is a SAVAK operation. The Officer in Charge is one Colonel Farshid Salehrad, as ruthless and unprincipled a bastard as ever was, and a true believer in the Islamic Republic. He has eight SAVAK regulars working for him at the prison. Two women from town are there during the daylight hours to cook and clean, but they leave the place every night."

"That's good stuff, Moe," said Cuthbert, "but we still don't know which of the buildings in or around Konarak is Qajar prison."

"Relax, Charles, I was getting to that," Rosenszweig replied. "Qajar prison sits pretty much off by itself on the outskirts of Konarak. It's located southwest of the old town at decimal coordinates 25.357-014, 60.388-935. Write them down." He repeated the numbers, even though he was sure the conversation was being recorded. "I recommend you get a surveillance drone over that facility, immediately. It's relatively small, less than seven hundred square meters per floor, with a basement and two stories above ground. The top level is supposed to be living quarters. The ground floor is for kitchen and dining, but also has some rooms which could be used as offices or possibly interrogation rooms. There's a walled-in courtyard in the back, where there are toilets, showers, a storage shed, and a generator."

Cuthbert listened intently, as Rosenszweig continued. "We are fairly certain the prisoners are being held in the basement. We were not able to actually get anyone into the basement, but when the shah ran the place, the basement had four rooms. The largest was fitted with two large iron cages. They are still there as far as we know. The shah used the three remaining smaller rooms to extract information from his prisoners, but we have no information about them beyond that."

"You mean the smaller rooms are torture chambers," Jones acknowledged.

"Most probably."

"Anything about security at the prison, Moe?" asked Siebert. "Any unusual military activity in the area?"

"There appears to be absolute confidence on the part of the Iranians that nobody outside of the government knows where your people are being held," Rosenszweig said. "And, other than evicting the locals and staffing Qajar with SAVAK regulars, they have done nothing to call attention to themselves. So, no, there has been no out-of-the-ordinary military activity in the area. There does not even appear to be a perimeter guard on the building."

"That's good news," Siebert said. "The more confident they are, the better for us. You'll tell us right away if you find out anything new?"

"Of course, Helen," Rosenszweig replied. "Your president is the best friend Israel has had in the White House in a decade," he added, "and rest assured we will do everything we can to make this operation—and his administration—a success."

18

Little Creek

Back in the briefing room, the map of the Gulf of Oman had been supplemented with enlarged satellite photographs of the Chabahar Bay area, and a larger map of the Persian Gulf and the Indian Ocean. There Porter and Clegg had assembled Jake, Cole, and four other SEALs from Jake's team: petty officers Fowles, Wilson, Bonsignore, and Janelli.

"Okay, here's the scoop," Cmdr. Porter said. "The code name for this evolution will be 'Operation Exodus.'"

Perfect, Jake thought. *Let my people go.* He pictured Charlton Heston holding up the stone tablets in *The Ten Commandments*. Moses. Like his cat.

Porter and Clegg briefly reviewed the information given to Jake and Cole the day before for the other men, and then Clegg continued, "Here's what we now know about Qajar Prison. Used to be the shah's provincial government headquarters, but was converted to a prison long before the Ayatollahs took over. The building's not that large, as you can see."

On the satellite picture, he pointed to a building on the outskirts of the city. "It's about one-and-a-half klicks [kilometers] from the beach at Chabahar bay, and just over four klicks south as you travel up this main road from the Gulf.

Any way we go in, they'll be no cover. You can see from the satellite picture there's just some scraggly palm trees and some low vegetation, but it's all mostly sand dunes and barren wasteland.

"The plan, remember," Clegg continued, "is to land on the south, gulf-side, beach. The big advantage of this particular route is less exposure at sea. The sub drops you off ten klicks from the beach, and that's the only waterborne exposure. About half-a-klick up from the beach there's this east-west perimeter road — parallels the shoreline." Clegg pointed again to the satellite photograph, "Here, coming off the perimeter road, and extending north, is the main road to Qajar.

"Now this north-south main road from the gulf climbs over these steep cliffs that border the entire area inland off the gulf." Clegg paused, eyes flitting from man to man. "Coming up from the beach, then, the quickest route to the prison is this main road. If, for any reason, you can't use the road to access the prison, then you may end up having to climb these here cliffs. Looks like a steep fifty-foot climb. So, by all means, stick to the road if at all possible."

"Now as to the prison itself," Porter said, taking the floor, "it's really not all that big. There are three levels, including the basement level, where we're pretty sure the prisoners are being held. Each level is about one hundred feet wide by seventy-five feet across — that's seventy-five-hundred square feet. The top level is supposed to be living quarters. The ground floor is for kitchen and dining, but also has some rooms which could be used as offices, or possibly interrogation rooms. The basement is where the shah housed his prisoners, and *that's* where SAVAK is most likely holding our people. It consists of one big room with two iron cages in it, and three other, smaller rooms. These might be prisoner cells, interview rooms, or even

113

torture chambers—we don't know. Again, our best estimate is that our people are being held somewhere in this underground complex.

"Off the ground floor is a small courtyard, forty-foot by seventy-five, with a gang latrine, showers, a shed of some sort, and a diesel generator. It's enclosed by a twelve-foot wall, topped with concertina wire.

"Ingress and egress to the building are by the front door only," Porter continued. "There's an exit to the flat roof from the second floor, and an exit to the courtyard from the ground floor, but they're dead ends. Each floor is accessed by a stairwell along the east wall. SAVAK has nine people on site, a colonel and eight regulars. Two women come in during the daylight hours to cook and clean, but they're not there at night.

"The Air Force is positioning drone surveillance over the site as we speak, so we'll have eyes-on during the operation."

"What's that, Commander, in the picture, just outside the complex?" Jake asked.

"I was just getting to that . . . *that*, Lieutenant, appears to be a 2017 Mercedes-Benz GLS, a cross between an SUV and a limo. What it's for, we're not sure, but best guess is that it belongs to the colonel."

"Guards?" Cole asked.

"Must be," Porter answered, "but these satellite pictures are only hours old, and they don't show anybody guarding the building from the outside. There's no evidence of any perimeter guard, and nobody outside on the roof, or guarding the entrance. The Iranians are either very lax, or very confident that we haven't a clue where, in their entire country, our people are being held. We can only surmise that any guarding of the building is being done from the inside."

Clegg took the floor again. "The plan is for the team to embark aboard the guided missile sub, *Carolina*, at Diego Garcia." (Cole winced. Riding in a submarine was not his favorite activity. Neither was it Jake's, but Jake had long since come to terms with his father and grandfather's favorite ride.)

"Unfortunately," Clegg continued. "DG is over two thousand miles away from your target, but DG is the closest really secure base we have for a submarine. Besides, *Carolina* can do the two thousand miles entirely submerged and completely undetected in just under three days. We can get you to DG pretty quick—less than a day. The good news is that any of the wet environment equipment you'll need is already forward-deployed to DG, and being loaded on *Carolina*, again, as we speak."

Cole looked at Jake and scowled. The idea of three days underwater made him *very* uncomfortable.

"Once off the coast from Konarak, you'll leave the sub underwater using its lockout system—a maneuver you guys have practiced at least half-a-dozen times—pump up the inflatable and board it on the surface, and then hit the beach under cover of darkness. Once in country, you'll be reporting to me right here, C2 [Command and Control], via encrypted satellite radio. The control team here will be in constant contact with the Air Force surveillance drone operator—they operate the damn things from Tempe, Arizona, for God's sake—again, by satellite. He or she will keep C2 advised as to any patrol boat activity on the way in to the beach. In fact, we'll maintain contact with the drone throughout the operation via satellite radio, right up until extraction. As to the extraction, we'll also have satellite radio contact with the carrier and the choppers."

"Those patrol boats operating on any kind of schedule?" Jake asked.

"We have no information about that at present. We'll know more when the Air Force gets their drones flying, and you'll know as soon as we do."

That," Jake thought, *is not very reassuring.*

"And the fishing fleet?" he asked, aloud.

"Their activities, at least, shouldn't affect the operation at all," Clegg said. "The fleet gets underway just before midnight and they fish all night. They return early in the morning, and process their catch. You gentlemen, on the other hand, will depart the sub at dusk, and should be ashore hours before the fishermen leave port.

"Okay, now," Clegg continued, "on landing, you'll ditch the inflatable and your underwater gear, transition to desert fatigues and field packs, and then go overland to the prison.

"When you reach the prison, then you go in, sweep the building, and secure the prisoners. Once the six 'packages' are secured, you'll alert C2 and we'll launch the helicopter team on the *Harry S. Truman*—the *Truman* being the carrier that's currently operating out in the Gulf. They will scramble three helicopters. The three choppers—a transport, a gunship, and a backup—will take a half hour, more or less, to get to the extraction point, and they can stay onsite for only a half hour more. So that's all the time you'll have to wrap up operations at the prison, and get to the extraction point.

"Needless to say, the sooner you get to the extraction site with the prisoners, the better. That's here, alongside this spot of greenery." He pointed to a spot on the satellite photo, "Two klicks due west, and away from, the prison." Clegg paused to consult his notes.

"Okay, radio call signs. You'll be using the satellite radiotelephones you're used to. C2 will be Exodus Base. Jake, you'll be Exodus Alfa. Cole, you're Exodus Bravo. You will have contact with the chopper pilots using the HF radio setting on the radiophones — use standard radio protocol. Again, there will be three choppers: one transport helo, Exodus One; a backup transport, Exodus Two; and a gunship, Exodus Three."

Clegg paused for effect. "So, the helicopter team from the *Truman*, arrives, everybody gets picked up, and they take you all home. Easy peasy."

Nobody laughed. *Easy peasy, my ass,* Jake thought. *Shit always happens.*

Porter then spoke up. "The rules of engagement, gentlemen, are simple. Anybody carrying a weapon is fair game. Otherwise, capture and secure in place. You'll be issued plenty of zip ties for just that purpose. Bottom line: Shoot to kill, but don't kill anybody you don't have to.

"Okay, gents, go straight to the Armorer. We've got some special equipment that ought to make the mission go a bit smoother. Dismissed!"

* * * * *

Unlike Army and Marine regulars, SEALs are not issued permanent weapons that they retain for their entire tour of duty — not even rifles. Instead they are issued weapons specific for each mission, and are expected to return them in good condition once the mission is complete.

The armorer was a CPO named Klink. While one would expect that anyone named Klink would be subject to some unmerciful ribbing, being compared to the German prison commandant of the same name in the old "Hogan's Heroes" TV series, nobody ever ribbed CPO Klink — about *anything.*

"Okay, men, Lieutenant," Klink said, "got some brand-new, gee-whiz gear for you. Now your standard flak jacket is worn outside your fatigues and is heavy as hell, right?"

The six SEALs nodded.

"Now this here," said Klink, who held up what looked very much like a vest made of the same material as a wet suit, "is worn inside your fatigues, a vest, but kinda like a tee shirt. It's made of a special carbon-fiber-reinforced Kevlar material, and it will stop a bullet up to .45 caliber, and it doesn't need a ceramic plate to do it. The carbon is in the form of something called nanotubes, which, I am told, converts a vertical force into a horizontal one, dissipating most all of the blow horizontally across the vest rather than vertically into your body. Not that you won't feel it of course, knock you right on your ass, but at least it won't pierce your skin. It's lighter," (he handed it to Cole) "'bout a quarter of the weight of a regular flak jacket. And it's even lined with a special material that wicks sweat away from your body, so it's almost as comfortable as a tee shirt. Still hot as hell, mind you, but nowhere near as bad as a flak jacket — okay?"

Jake and the rest nodded. Fowles spoke up. "Chief, this flimsy thing will stop a .45 round?"

"Wouldn't say it if it weren't true. Now take off your shirts and fit one to yourself. There's a bunch right here, sizes marked on 'em, just like the tee shirts at Walmart." He snickered. "Kinda gives a whole new meaning to the brand name 'Under Armour,' right?" he quipped, laughing aloud at his own joke.

Jake found a vest to fit him and put it on. As the chief had promised, it was light, but certainly much heavier and much hotter than a regular tee shirt. Too bad this mission wasn't to someplace cold, like Norway. It didn't have sleeves like a tee shirt, and apparently a panel in the back made that part double thick, but it still was something less than a half inch thick. The front of the vest was double breasted, with two panels folding over one another, held in place by Velcro strips. The double panels made the front of the vest the same thickness as the back. Okay, it made you feel hot, but, still, this jacket wasn't as uncomfortable as a flak jacket worn outside one's fatigues, and there were no ceramic plates to weigh you down. He noted that the front of the vest extended down further than a regular flak jacket covering his lower abdomen. *Too bad it doesn't go down far enough to protect the family jewels.* Suddenly he thought of Julie, then castigated himself for thinking about her right after thinking about the family jewels.

"Now," Klink continued, "next thing. Helmets. These will replace your standard issue. Same material as the vests, carbon-fiber-reinforced Kevlar with them nanotubes. Looks more like a football helmet than a combat helmet, right? And light." He tossed one to Jake, who marveled at its light weight. "And out-performs current issue. Again, each man will please get one sized to fit you."

Jake tried the new helmet on. It was larger than the old one, because its walls were thicker, yet it was still much lighter. The inside suspension mesh was pretty much the same, however.

After each of them had the new vests and helmets to fit, Klink grinned like a happy Santa Claus.

"And that, gentlemen, is all the *new* toys I have for you today. Wear them in good health! Now, for the normal stuff. First, your rifles. This trip, you get the M4a1, fully automatic. Shorter and sweeter than the standard M4—just perfect for close-in work. And don't forget your ammo. Three high-cap clips per man, one mounted and two spares. Standard 5.56 mm NATO rounds."

Klink continued. "For you, Fowles, as demolitions expert, you get to haul around the demolition charges, flash-bang grenades, and flares. Wilson, you get a field medical kit. And, for each of you, some night vision gear. And three satellite radiotelephones. One for the Lieutenant, and one for the Chief, and one to grow on. Don't forget to keep the batteries charged. A charge is supposed to hold for seventy-two hours, but I wouldn't bank on it. Here are some zip-tie bundles — always handy to have around for securing prisoners. Also, one Ka-Bar each, and one wad of money — a thousand U.S. dollars' worth of euros. The Iranian *rial* isn't worth shit, and hard currency rules," Klink finally concluded.

"You hold the cash, Billy," Jake ordered.

"You mean you want me to sign for it," Cole said, displeased.

"I do," Jake said, pleased with himself. Even so, he and the others had to sign for each item of the other equipment they had received as well.

19

Broken

Konarak

Clare Tindal knew she could almost set her watch by her period. She was never late, unless . . . She had been late only three times before, and, each time, the pregnancy had ended in miscarriage. She should have begun her period a week or so after they were arrested, and while she was uncertain as to exactly how long ago that was, she was dead certain that her period should have long since begun. No, she was pregnant, she was sure of it.

Of course, her husband could well be the father. She hoped that such was the case. But she had also been raped again and again since her capture, and (she shuddered involuntarily at the thought) either Screwtape or Wormwood could well be the father of her child. If so, then so be it. If she did carry a child in her womb, it was totally innocent, and in no way responsible for the circumstances surrounding its conception, whatever they were. No, this was *her* child, and she would do whatever was necessary to carry *her* child to term. *Even* if it meant betraying her country.

After her last session with the colonel, he had not immediately returned her to the cage to rejoin the others. Nor had he just left her in the interrogation room overnight, as he had done many times before. Instead, he had given her a bar of soap, a clean towel, and a clean prison uniform, brought her up the stairs and out into the courtyard, into the daylight. And he left her there, alone, saying, "Enjoy the shower at your leisure. When you're ready, knock on the door. There will be a meal waiting for you."

Bathed, in a clean uniform dress, and with a full belly for the first time in forever, Clare was returned by the colonel to the underground cage with the other two women. She suddenly realized how squalid the place really was, and how overwhelming its stink. Filthy bodies and human excrement.

* * * * *

Clare Tindal was born Clare Longstreet. The Longstreets owned a small farm just outside of Vicksburg, Mississippi, and Clare had been their only child. Her mother made sure Clare dressed and acted like a lady in public, especially in church every Sunday, but her father treated her as the son he never had. He would take her hunting and fishing with him, and, truth be told, while she never particularly enjoyed either activity, she was very good at them, relishing the time with her father.

Robert Longstreet, Clare's father, had served as a State Senator for four years, when his party leadership had asked him to run for Congress. He was elected Representative for Mississippi's 26th District when Clare was just twelve, and had been reelected every two years since.

Clare killed her first deer at thirteen. She had sighted the buck first, and pointed him out to her father, home from DC for the weekend. But he told her that she had seen it first, and therefore it was her kill. She had practiced with a rifle since she was ten, and had become a better-than-fair marksman, so she downed the buck easily. Less easy was her father's insistence that she then clean and butcher the animal (with his help, of course). She discovered that gutting and cleaning a fish was easy in comparison, but she was, after all, a farm girl, and she was knew well where the meat that she and her family ate came from. Every hunting season after that, save one, and up until she married and left home, she had bagged a deer.

She was also a bright student, with a gift for both language and mathematics. After high school, her parents encouraged her to attend college, and she selected, and was accepted at, Mississippi College, a small Christian university affiliated with the Mississippi Baptist Convention. Mississippi College was also close to home, in nearby Clinton, Mississippi. To save on expenses, she could live at home and commute to school. Her parents bought her a used Nissan Sentra with 146,000 miles on it.

Clare thoroughly enjoyed her college experience. There was a beautiful campus, all green trees and lush lawns, the facilities both steeped in history (founded 1826) and immaculate. Clare majored in English and minored in math, and she did very well.

It was while she was at Mississippi College that she met and, after graduation, married, John Tindal. John was from Corinth, Mississippi, and had majored in secondary education. After graduation, he got a job teaching high school in Farmington, Mississippi, and Clare got an administrative job in the same high school. It was in Farmington that they joined the Church of the Good News. The rest, as they say, was history.

20

En Route to Diego Garcia

It was 9,700-or-so miles to Diego Garcia from Virginia. Jake and his team boarded the huge Boeing C-17 Globemaster III at Langley Air Force Base, a five-hour car ride north from Little Creek.

The Air Force lieutenant colonel who piloted the beast was surprised to find that his cargo was just six men with full pack. His two hundred million dollar-plus aircraft, after all, was designed to carry a hundred and thirty troops and all their equipment.

"You guys must have some important work to do," he volunteered, eyeing their M4a1 special operations rifles and night-vision gear. Jake started to say something, but the pilot held up his hand and said, "No, I don't want to know, Lieutenant. It's probably way above my pay grade, anyway. Strap in, guys. I can't promise you comfort, but I can promise you wheels down in Diego Garcia in about twelve hours. The weather looks good, and we're cleared to thirty-eight thousand feet, all the way to DG. Sleep if you can, but there's no smoking. There's some coffee and some sandwiches and snacks forward, just aft of the cockpit, and you're welcome to them. See you in DG." With that, he gave them a sloppy salute and went forward to join the rest of the aircraft's crew.

"Doesn't seem like such a bad guy for a cake-eater," Cole volunteered. The team members snickered. SEALs considered themselves vastly superior to any other military unit, and especially looked down on anything Air Force. An Air Force Combat Control Team, Jake knew, might give them an argument.

"Now, now, Chief," Jake said, "remember that the cake-eaters and us, we all report to the same CINC [Commander-In-Chief]." Cole scowled. The current CINC was ever a sore subject with Billy Cole.

Once in the air, Jake leaned back into the seriously uncomfortable jump seat the aircraft provided and surveyed his team. Everyone else was struggling to get comfortable. Billy Cole was already sound asleep. CPO William Cole had been his alter ego on four previous missions, and the burly African-American had never once disappointed him. Jake knew that Billy Cole always "had his six."

Over the two years they had worked together, Jake had been a frequent visitor to the Cole home, and his two kids, William, Jr. and Kelly, referred to him as "Uncle Jake." Jake regarded Cole's wife, Emma, somewhat in awe. She accepted Cole's role as a SEAL, dangerous as it was, and seemed ready for anything, just the way his own mother and grandmother were. And now Jake wondered if his current love interest, Julie O'Leary, was that kind of woman.

Special Warfare Operator First Class (SO1) Foster Fowles was twenty-six years old, single, and had spent all of his life, after graduating high school, in the Navy. Blonde, of average height and build, his physical capabilities were still a match for anyone on the team. Fowles was, as was every other member of the team, an expert marksman. He was also a demolition and explosives expert. Every Navy SEAL is required to take twelve weeks of "total immersion" language training, and, as a result, Fowles spoke fluent Pashto. He had done two tours in Afghanistan, his last one with Jake and Billy Cole at Conciliation Base, embedded with the Marine Corps, in Kandahar Province.

SO1 Clarence "Slewfoot" Wilson, also twenty-six, divorced with no children, was tall and lanky. His regular easy-going demeanor belied a dogged tenacity under fire. Wilson had combat medical training, and was an Arabic speaker. He had also served with Jake and Cole in Afghanistan.

SO2 Jerry Bonsignore was also with Jake in Afghanistan. Bonsignore was heavy-set and balding, but was probably the most athletically-capable man on the team. At thirty, married with two children, he was also its oldest enlisted member after Chief Cole. Bonsignore had studied Russian.

SO3 Leo Janelli, at twenty-four, was the youngest member of the team. Still single, Janelli was short and thin, and could outrun any SEAL at Little Creek. He had been trained in jungle warfare, but had yet to put his training to the test. Janelli spoke Spanish, and had also served with Jake and Cole in Afghanistan.

Just under twelve hours later, the team was deposited at the British Indian Ocean Territory Diego Garcia, just as the USAF lieutenant colonel had promised. An hour-and-a-half later, they were aboard the USS Carolina, en route to points north.

21

Disunity

Konarak

Mary Rogers and Adele Crowley were nonplussed by the change in Clare Tindal. They were, of course, surprised, and a bit envious, when Clare had been returned to their cage freshly bathed and in a clean prison uniform. But when they asked what had happened, Clare assured them that she had remained steadfast and had resisted the Colonel's latest tactics, just as well she had resisted his old ones.

But Clare had changed nonetheless. She was—*set apart*—there was no other way to put it. She was no longer an integral part of the group. Now, she seemed somehow secretive—even from her husband. While she continued to say and do all the right things, she seemed to have lost her spirit, her will to resist, this the result of some special knowledge the rest of them were not party to.

Now, instead of supporting the firm resolve of the group to reject every overture from the colonel, Clare argued that there could be no harm in at least being civil to the man. Humoring the colonel, and at least *appearing* to give a sympathetic ear to his overtures, she now suggested, could be of immediate benefit to all of them. After all, just by appearing to consider his overtures, Clare had earned a bath, a clean uniform, and a full meal. Wouldn't an end to the torture, some adequate food, a shower and some clean clothing, be worth some insignificant conciliatory gesture on their part?

At first, John Tindal and the other two couples argued with Clare, urging her to return to her former resolve, to maintain the group's solidarity. But their maltreatment continued, and while the others were still dragged from the cages at regular intervals for interrogation in the following three days, Clare was not.

Adele Crowley had been the first to break ranks from the others and ask Clare what she had to do to get some respite from ill treatment. As near as she could remember, Clare related her experience at her last session with the colonel. "All I did was listen," she said, "and not give him any of the reasons why I could never do the things he was asking me to do. You know, Adele, I think he really does think we were here to spy on them. And while I admitted to nothing, I didn't deny anything either, and that seemed to satisfy him. And at least I got a shower, clean clothing, and a decent meal out of the deal. Although now," she quipped, "I'd be civil to him again for just another decent meal."

She would soon be given her chance.

22

Under the Arabian Sea

The Nuclear Guided Missile Submarine (SSGN) *Carolina* was, as were other four other boats in her class, a converted *Ohio*-class Ballistic Missile Nuclear Submarine (SSBN).

The START II Strategic Arms Reduction Treaty limited the number of ballistic missile boats that could remain in service. Rather than decommission the excess of those vessels in service at the time, the Navy proposed, and Congress agreed, to convert these boats to launch cruise missiles instead. As part of that conversion, the forward two vertical launch tubes were to be turned into lockout chambers, enabling special operations forces and their equipment to exit the vessel submerged. Dedicated onboard accommodations and facilities for special forces were also planned. *Carolina's* conversion, at General Dynamics Electric Boat's Groton, Connecticut, facility, took three years and cost $150 million. The work was completed in December, 2008.

Once *Carolina* was underway, had reached the 100-fathom curve off Diego Garcia, and submerged, Jake and Cole inspected the equipment that had already been loaded onto the sub. They were gratified to find that all the necessary wet gear was there. Included were wet suits in various sizes, masks, snorkels, chemical glow sticks, and water- and pressure-proof flashlights.

To stay as quiet as possible, no outboard motor would be used on the rubber boat going in to the beach; instead, four paddles were stored with the inflatable boat. The team would use muscle power for what was planned to be a short run to the beach.

The gear they brought with them on the C-17, fatigues, weapons, their armored undershirts, night vision equipment, the upscale helmets, boots, bundles of zip ties, and so forth, were already loaded into watertight bags to be towed behind them as the exited the sub. In three of those bags, the satellite radiotelephones would be carried. The radiotelephones could reach, via the secure DOD communications satellite, from point-to-point, anywhere on the globe. A separate setting allowed line-of-sight and short distance HF radio communication between units in the field. While currently on charge, the radios would to be taken off charge and stowed away just before the team exited the boat. A charge was, as Chief Klink had said, supposed to be good for seventy-two hours.

The watertight bag that Fowles, the team's demolition expert, would tow behind was somewhat larger. It contained demolition charges, flash-bang grenades, and flares. Slewfoot Wilson's bag, was also just a bit larger. It contained a field medical kit. Cole's was not no bigger, but it did hold the thousand dollars' worth of euros. (The Iranian *rial*, supposedly legal tender throughout the Islamic Republic, was subject to hyperinflation and decreased in value against hard currencies continuously. As a result, though officially illegal, all cash business in Iran was usually done in U.S. dollars or euros.)

* * * * *

Jake was helping himself to coffee in the wardroom, when *Carolina's* commanding officer, Commander Jarvis Proteus, "J.P." Helfenstein, joined him with the same intent. It was their first day out, and *Carolina* was at 350 feet and steaming north-northwest at flank speed. Helfenstein, Jake thought, and despite the fatigue-type uniform, looked more like a prosperous lawyer than a submarine commander.

"Hello, Lieutenant," he said, extending his hand. "I'm J.P. Helfenstein."

"Yessir, Captain, your reputation precedes you, and I'm very pleased to meet you."

"And I you, Mr. Lawlor. Your father and grandfather are pretty much legends in the submarine service."

"Yessir, so I've been told, many, many times. And I'm immensely proud of both of them."

"Sure you are," he said. "And I'm sure you've been asked this question before — not that the trident pinned to your chest isn't impressive — so how come *you're* not wearing dolphins?"

"Lotsa reasons," Jake replied, smiling, "but mostly, I think, it goes back to the day my grandfather took me on a tour of a WWII boat like the one he drove in the Pacific."

"Go on," Helfenstein said, his interest piqued.

"Dad was CO of the *Edison* at the time, and we were stationed at Kings Bay, Georgia. I remember I was about eleven, and my grandparents had come for a visit — I think it was over the fourth — and Grandpa and Grandma hijacked us kids and drove us up to Patriots Point in South Carolina to see the 'South Carolina Navy.' "

"Been there," Helfenstein said. "They have the carrier *Yorktown*; a destroyer; the submarine *Clamagore*; the NS

131

Savannah, used to be there, but it's gone now. All museum ships, as I recall."

"Yessir . . . well, I thought the *Yorktown* was really cool, especially the vintage aircraft they had lashed down to the flight deck and all, but then Grandpa took us on a guided tour of the sub."

"And?"

"And I couldn't believe that my grandfather had made a dozen war patrols in what I saw as a length of sewer pipe jammed full of pipes and valves and gauges. I imagined some seventy men jammed aboard the boat all at once, and went claustrophobic. I couldn't wait to get the blazes out of the thing."

Helfenstein laughed aloud. "And do submarines still make you claustrophobic?"

"No, Sir, not now, and, *please*, don't forget I was only eleven at the time! I'd been aboard the nuke boats my dad commanded before that, and they *never* affected me the way the *Clamagore* did that day. After all, Captain, if I was claustrophobic, I would hardly be able to sit calmly in an enclosed escape hatch while it was being flooded."

"Good point," Helfenstein agreed.

"I'm certainly comfortable enough here in *Carolina,*" Jake continued, "but I'll freely admit that I'd always choose to be outside in the open air, and not cooped up underwater, given the choice. Your boat's amazing, Sir, the accommodations are first class, and the chow is fantastic. But the idea of living underwater for weeks on end just isn't for me."

"And all the while breathing amine-laced air with only 16% oxygen. No, I get it. Subs are not for everyone. So why not the surface navy, then?"

"In *my* family, Sir? You've got to be kidding! Bad enough I'm a SEAL—at least that makes me halfway acceptable—but if I'd gone surface warfare, I'd have been disowned entirely. My grandfather would always say 'There's just submarines and targets.' "

"I hear that," Helfenstein said, grinning. "I *do* hear that. But it must have been great growing up in that environment. Your grandfather was the model Naval officer. His exploits in *Orca* during the war are the stuff of legend—part of the required curriculum at sub school. That's not to say that your dad doesn't have a rep as well—just not as colorful. They both must have told some great sea stories!"

"They did, that—my grandfather especially. My dad less so, because much of what he did was still classified. They did have some interesting arguments, though. Grandpa was teed off that the Navy had phased out conventional boats. He was adamant that there was still a role for them to play. Dad, however, was just as adamant that there was nothing a submarine had to do that a nuclear sub couldn't do, and do it better than any boat that had to continually come up for air."

"Well," Helfenstein said, "your grandfather actually did have a point—especially today, with the new AIP boats."

"AIP. That's Air Independent Propulsion, right?"

"Correct. The nukes have fuel enough for years and years, but fuel was never the limiting factor for subs. The need to breathe air was the thing tying them to the surface. The World War Two boats carried enough fuel comfortably to give them a range of ten thousand miles. No, ability to stay submerged was limited by one thing alone: in a word, *air*. They needed air for the men to breathe, and more critically, they needed air for propulsion—in the case of the World War Two fleet subs, air for their diesels to breathe.

133

"The nuclear boats solved the problem of air for the crew to breathe early on by manufacturing and refreshing the air in the boat," Helfenstein continued, "and that technology was completely transferrable to conventionally-powered boats. But adding to that, the Japanese and the Europeans are building AIP boats today with propulsion systems and advanced batteries that allow them to remain submerged for up to three weeks."

"Three weeks," Jake said, "I should think that would be long enough for a great many of the jobs subs are called upon to do."

"Exactly," Helfenstein agreed. "And they're also cheaper. You can buy five AIP boats for what *Carolina* would cost to build today. And quieter. They can also go places a nuke *can't* go, because they displace only a quarter to a third of what *Carolina* does. So they're even more undetectable than the quietist nuclear boats."

"Whoa," Jake laughed. "And *you're* the skipper of a nuke? Doesn't that amount to some kind of heresy?"

"Maybe it does," Helfenstein smiled back, "but last winter, at BALTOPS, we operated in the Baltic with NATO naval and air units. The average depth in the Baltic Sea is a hundred and eighty-five feet, and we had a hell of a time maneuvering the boat. We couldn't get anywhere near the shoreline. But let me tell you, the German AIP boat operating with us, *U-35*, was powered by fuel cells. It could go all the places we couldn't, stayed submerged for the whole two weeks, and could have stayed down another whole week if it wanted to. And, unlike us, it went undetected the whole time."

"So why don't we build any of these boats?" Jake asked.

"Navy mindset," Helfenstein opined. "Goes back to [Vice Admiral Hyman] Rickover. The admiral had a closed mind when it came to anything other than nuclear propulsion for submarines, and, at the time, his mindset was completely justified. *Nautilus* was, after all, head and shoulders above the best diesel-electric boat in service at the time. But times change, and the Navy brass hasn't."

"Surely somebody upstairs will take notice," Jake allowed. "Perhaps these boats just haven't been in service long enough to get their attention."

Helfenstein laughed aloud. "I don't know what more it would take to change their minds, Jake," he said. "Back in 2014, the Navy actually took out a two-year lease on one of the first AIP boats, along with its crew. The boat was Swedish, the *Gotland,* and it conducted exercises with the fleet in San Diego. The *Gotland* more than proved its capability by staying underwater for two weeks at a time, remaining completely undetected, and 'sinking' the carrier *Ronald Reagan* a bunch of times. If that didn't get the attention of the powers that be, I don't know what will."

And Jake had no answer for that. But then he didn't have to. He had chosen, after all, *not* to be a submariner.

23

A Chink in the Armor

Konarak

Once again Clare Tindal sat across the table from the colonel. Given the perpetual daylight in the cage, Clare thought that it had been almost a week earlier, but just three days had passed since their last interview. Salehrad smelled victory.

"Well, Clare," he asked, "have you thought about what we discussed the last time?"

"I have," she said, "And I want to know what will happen to me and to the others if we say what you want to hear."

"You mean if you decide to admit the truth?" he asked, speaking gently.

"You know what I mean," she said.

"How can I know that?" Salehrad said. "I would never ask you to say anything other than what you know to be true. I would never do that." He paused. "So, Clare, have you and your friends been spying on the Islamic Republic?"

"I don't think so, but after what we talked about last time, I'm not so sure," she replied.

"What is it you're not sure of?" he asked.

"I'm not sure of what you mean by spying."

"Not sure," he echoed. "What do you think it means to be a spy?"

Clare was silent for a while, but the colonel waited her out. Finally, she felt impelled to speak, if, for nothing else, to fill the void in the conversation. "You know," she replied, "observing troop movements and such, and reporting them back to someone at home . . ."

"And what was it you were doing? Weren't you observing?"

"Not really," she replied. "We were spreading the Gospel of Jesus Christ."

"And were you not sensing the mood of the people? Looking for their responses to your preaching? Iran is an *Islamic* republic. Were you not seeing if you could or could not pry the Iranian people away from their belief in Islam?"

"Of course we were," she said. "That's how you spread the Gospel!"

"And were you not reporting your progress daily? Reporting to your pastor back in the U.S.?"

"Well . . . yes, we were supposed to, but we only got the chance to do that a couple times before you arrested us, and that was even before we even started preaching: you arrested us off the street on our first day of preaching."

Salehrad ignored her equivocation and pressed on. "And did you know that your pastor has been in regular contact with a congressman?" he said. *A bit of distortion, perhaps,* Salehrad thought, *but I know they've talked at least once . . .*

"Not regular contact, no," Clare said, interrupting his thought. "Our pastor knows congressmen who represent our state, sure. Like Representative Longstreet, for instance. And so they talk once in a while. They're friends. Why, Longstreet's a fine Christian man!"

137

No, I didn't know all that, but I'll take it, the colonel thought. "And, of course, Clare, we do know that Robert Longstreet *is also your father.* So everything you reported to your pastor was passed directly to your father – to the U.S. government! How is it, then, that this was not spying?"

They know! Clare thought, panicked. *They know my dad's a congressman!* She fought back her surprise, fought to regain her composure.

"That's ridiculous... We passed on nothing of any consequence . . ."

"And how do you *know* that? Do you know what information, exactly, your team passed on?"

"Not everything, no . . . no, not exactly."

"I thought as much. Clare, do you not see how you have become a victim here? You are suffering because of what you have become involved in. And your father and your government has left you hanging out to dry."

"No, my father would never do that! He wouldn't!"

"Wouldn't he?" The colonel raised his voice just a bit. "Then why has your father and your government left you here to rot? To be beaten, debased, and abused? Is it possibly because they have involved you in this scheme, and now don't know how to get you out of it? And what about the others – just how much have they been telling you?" He paused to let all this bit of illogic sink in. "And the Islamic Republic, which is only fighting for its national security, has been forced to resort to drastic measures to foil this plot—a plot in which you and your companions are implicitly involved."

Clare felt pregnant and exhausted, her body violated and still bearing bruises. She was once again hungry and dirty, *and* was now also thoroughly confused. She sat for a full minute without speaking.   Finally, she said, "So what is it you want me to do? How can I make all of this stop?"

And so he told her.

24

Getting There

Arabian Sea

It was their first full day at sea. Working with *Carolina's* Chief of the Boat (COB), a senior chief petty officer with twenty-eight years' service, Jake and his team practiced exiting the boat and deploying their gear. The team familiarized themselves with the peculiarities of *Carolina's* lockout systems. Both lockout trunks would be used, each accommodating three men and their equipment. They practiced finding their way inside the chambers in the dark, memorizing particularly the location and use of the onboard breathing equipment, which they would use while the lockout trunks were being flooded. Once flooded, the upper hatch would be opened to the sea, the inflatable would be released from the port chamber, and the team members would free rise to the surface, towing their individual equipment behind.

The COB insisted on spreading the inflatable out on the deck and having the team, blindfolded, go through the motions of finding the paddles and the bottle of compressed gas that would inflate the craft. They practiced stowing their towed equipment on board the inflatable. Cole and Jake would then open their watertight bags, extract their M4a1s, secure their bags, and then stand guard while the others simulated rowing to the beach.

"That was excellent," the COB said after the second time around. "Now let's do it again."

When they were done practicing, they pored over the maps they had brought aboard with them and reviewed their plans. Later in the day the team made full use of the well-equipped gym aboard *Carolina*.

At 1400 local time, *Carolina* was brought up to what would have been periscope depth if *Carolina* had a periscope (her periscope having been long since replaced with electronic cameras mounted on retractable masts external to the pressure hull), there to receive a daily radio broadcast. The broadcast included an Exodus-priority message from Little Creek C2, to be relayed to Jake and his team. It contained new information gathered from drone surveillance over the target site:

USAF drone controllers report eleven people coming and going from the prison building. Two of these individuals vacate the place at night and ride bicycles into town, then come back in the morning. These two daytime staff would be the cleaning and cooking crew, whereas eight of remaining nine individuals appear to live onsite. One person, designated "VIP" by drone controllers, travels back and forth by automobile to a building in town, grid coordinates 25.359-214, 60.395-476, identified as a hotel. Subject VIP travels to and from at irregular intervals, apparently in residence there. No observed patrol boat activity outside Chabahar Bay.

* * * * *

Jake would have preferred eating his meals with his team in the crew's mess, but naval shipboard protocol required that he take his meals with the other officers in the wardroom. That evening, after dinner, Jake and Commander Helfenstein sat talking.

"We're making good time, Jake," Helfenstein volunteered. "We departed Diego Garcia just over thirty hours ago, and we're already almost halfway to the target area. 'Ole' *Carolina* is really haulin' ass! At this rate we'll be just off Chabahar Bay well before dusk the day after tomorrow—in about thirty-six hours."

"That's outstanding, Captain," Jake said. "We *are* making good time. Any updated news as to the weather at the site?"

"Same-old, same-old, Jake. Typical south Iran winter day, hot and humid, no precipitation predicted. No wind to speak of. The sea should be like glass when you hit the surface."

"That's both good and bad news. We should have little trouble with the inflatable and loading our gear, but we'll be sitting ducks for any Iranian Navy patrol boat that just happens to be passing by."

"The Air Force drone jockeys haven't been able to establish any pattern there?" Helfenstein asked.

"No pattern whatsoever, apparently. But they *have* said that so far the Iranian boats pretty much stay in the bay. We can only hope that they'll stay there and not decide to venture out to sea on the night we arrive."

"Hope is not a plan," Helfenstein intoned.

"Book by that name, isn't there, Sir?" Jake said, smiling.

"Yep. Read it. Actually, I think, it's a collection of articles by a bunch of people, all about how we screwed up in Iraq by going in there without any clear exit plan."

"Well, Sir," Jake said, "we've actually got a pretty decent exit plan for Operation Exodus. It's our entrance plan and what we'll be doing when we get onsite that leaves a little bit to be desired."

"And that doesn't bother you?" Helfenstein asked, genuinely concerned.

"Hell yes, it does, Sir. But we're SEALs. If we're issued lemons, we make lemonade."

More balls than brains, Helfenstein thought, but said nothing. *But then, I* did *opt out of joining the Marine Corps second class year at the Academy, and most Marines think submariners are bonkers.*

* * * * *

Later that same evening, Jake was hanging out with his team outside the special ops bunkroom, when, aside, he asked Cole, "How does Emma do it, Billy?"

"Do What?"

"Put up with all of this. I come from a military family that came from a military family, and the strength of the women who 'stood and waited' for their men has always mystified me. So how does Emma do it?"

"Hell if I know, Jake. She just does." He paused in thought for a few seconds. "I mean she knew what she signed on for when she married me." Then he grinned, and puffed his chest out a bit. "But then again, I'm worth it, ain't I?"

"C'mon, Billy, I'm serious. I'm not sure I could ever ask a woman to put up with our kind of life. Six months in Afghanistan, and now we take off for Iran at the drop of a hat. And what we do is dangerous. Between the roadside bombs in Kandahar, the Taliban nutcases, and now extracting abducted American citizens from a prison fortress in Iran . . . I mean we knew all that up front when *we* signed on, and we've been trained for it, but the families—your *family*, your *wife*—they may have *thought* they knew what they were getting into, but

143

could they really? They must know that there's every possibility that one day you'll be coming home in an aluminum box."

"Guess I never thought about it that way," admitted Billy. "But Emma and the kids seem to be hanging in there. And there's never any guarantee, no matter what any of us does for a living, that we won't get hit by a bus or catch a stray bullet in the 'hood. Leastwise in *my* old 'hood. But what brought all of this on?"

Jake didn't answer.

Cole mulled all of it over for a bit. "It's your girlfriend Julie, ain't it?" It was more of a statement than a question.

"What? No, of course not. And Julie's not my girlfriend. We're just very good friends. More like a little sister to me, you know?"

"If you really do think about her like that, Jake, then you're a lot dumber than I thought."

"What are you getting at, Billy?"

"Just this. Julie likes you, though 'like' may be too weak a word here. And you know it, too, even if you can't admit it to yourself. And what's more, you like her right back, and just as much. Hell, I can see it just the couple times I've seen the two of you together."

"You're wrong, Billy. That's not true at all."

"Right. And you don't *ever* think about her."

"Of course I do," Jake said. And it dawned on him that he thought about her pretty often. "After all, she watches my cat."

Cole laughed aloud. "Your *cat*? And that's the only reason you think about her?"

"Okay, other reasons, too. And why is it so funny that she watches my cat for me?"

"What's funny is that you think the only reason she watches your cat for you is that she likes your cat."

And Jake, suddenly lost in thought, had no comeback.

25

Defection

Konarak

Clare Tindal never returned to the cage. That in itself was not unusual in the short term, but became a concern to the others after what appeared to them to be an entire day. John Tindal was beside himself.

They didn't know it, but Clare had been whisked off to the hotel in town where Salehrad was staying, and had been set up in the room adjoining his suite on the building's third floor. It had a real shower and an actual toilet, and a bed with clean sheets.

When she was left alone in the room, the door locked behind her, she first gorged on the bowl of fresh fruit that had been left on the round table next to her bed, and then shed her filthy prison uniform and took a long, hot shower. When she came out of the bathroom, the uniform was gone, a meal had been set on the table, and a folded stack of plain-looking street clothes had been placed at the foot of the bed. The hotel staff — if it *was* the hotel staff — had done a fairly good job of guessing her clothing sizes, and had even provided an industrial-grade bra, some granny panties, and a nightgown to sleep in. She would win no beauty contests in those clothes, but they were at least clean and dry. And nothing was colored orange.

And the meal was excellent.

With Clare absent, the colonel now concentrated his attentions on Adele Crowley, and told Screwtape and Wormwood that henceforward they had permission to physically abuse only the remaining woman, Mary Rogers.

And the sound equipment had finally arrived from Teheran. Now, added to the constant bright lights, was an endless loop of the same five Iranian *al-baloshi* songs. The music featured wailing singers accompanied by *dotars*, long-necked, two-string lutes, and was played at maximum volume.

The aural assault had been endured for some time when Adele Crowley, back from a session with the colonel, returned to the cages cleaned up and with a full belly. Not long afterwards, the guards reappeared and dragged John Tindal from the men's cage, and into an interrogation room. There the music could still be heard in the background, but in the sealed, cement-walled, room it was more like annoying elevator music — but louder. Salehrad sat, smoking, apparently oblivious to the undulating music. Tindal was forcibly seated in the chair across the table from him, and the hood and handcuffs were removed.

"How are you holding up, John?" the colonel asked, sounding actually concerned.

"What have you done with my wife?" Tindal demanded, ignoring the question.

"I can assure you, John, Clare is just fine," Salehrad answered calmly,

"I want to see her." Belligerent.

"In due time, John, in due time. But let us talk a bit first, shall we?" And the Colonel spoke to his prisoner with much

147

the same line of reasoning that he had used with Clare Tindal and Adele Crowley, and which, indeed, he had used with all the others. Unlike Clare and Adele, though, and despite his precarious mental and physical state, John Tindal was not yet buying, not even after he found out that the colonel knew all about his father-in-law.

Finally, after what seemed an eternity to Tindal, but was actually less than an hour, Salehrad said "Very well, John, would you like to visit Clare now?"

"I would," Tindal replied, still belligerent.

"But she is not here, John. I shall have to take you to her." He then summoned the guards in Farsi. When the guards entered the room, they again cuffed Tindal and put a blackout hood back over his head. Instead of ordering his return to the cage, however, Tindal understood the colonel to order the guard to take him "upstairs and out to the car."

On the drive to the hotel, John Tindal tried to memorize the route. He counted off the seconds it took to reach the first turn, noted the direction, the seconds to the next . . . And then the Colonel said, "I think, John, that when you see Clare, you'll be pleasantly surprised," and Tindal lost his train of thought. Soon thereafter, the car came to a stop. There was the sound of passing traffic — street noises.

"Take off the hood and the handcuffs," Tindal heard the colonel order in Farsi, and the guard sitting next to him obeyed. In a teaching moment, he said to the guard, "Never attract undue attention, the Israelis have spies everywhere."

Tindal was at first blinded by the sunlight, but he noted that the colonel had been driving, and there was only the one guard with him. They had stopped in front of an older, pretentious-looking building. It took up most of the city block on what was a busy, wide boulevard. The sign over the building entrance was in Persian script, which he could not read, but there was, underneath the script, one word in English: "Hotel."

The colonel nodded to the desk clerk on the way in, and the clerk proffered a set of keys. Taking them, Salehrad led the other two men up two flights of stairs and down the hall to the right. Tindal recognized another one of the colonel's men standing guard in front of the next-to-the-last door at the end of the hall on the left. The guard stepped aside as the Colonel unlocked the room and ushered Tindal inside. Salehrad closed the door behind him, leaving both guards outside in the hallway.

Clare stood up as the men entered the room. "Clare!" Tindal exclaimed.

"John?" she said. She noted that he looked worse than she had ever seen him—emaciated and dirty. And he stank of body odor and human excrement.

"Are you all right?" he asked, noting that she was dressed in street clothes, and that she was clean, her hair in order.

"I'm fine," she said. There was a bowl of fresh fruit on the table next to her. She picked it up, and glanced at the colonel, who, unseen to Tindal, nodded in approval. "Here," she said, offering the bowl, "have something to eat." Tindal grabbed a pear and devoured it, the juice running down his face and fingers. "You poor dear," Clare said.

Later, John Tindal sat beside his wife as Salehrad sat across the room, observing. "What have you done? What have you admitted to?" he asked, whispering, accusing.

"I've done nothing, admitted to nothing . . . Nothing that wasn't true," she said. "I haven't told the Colonel that I—we—did anything that we did not, in fact, actually do."

"Like what?"

149

"I've admitted that we were in Teheran to be among the Iranian people. That we were there to preach the Gospel."

"And ?"

"I don't know what you mean."

"And to what else did you admit, Clare?"

"I admitted that we reported to our Pastor daily, telling him our progress. About the Iranian peoples' reaction to us. How we reported they were afraid to talk to us about Jesus, and wouldn't take any of the Bibles we brought with us."

"But we could never have reported that, not to the Pastor, nor to anyone else. They arrested us on our first day out in the street."

"Perhaps not," Clare replied, eyes downcast. "But we would have if we could. I told the colonel only what was true, that we were supposed to report back on whatever progress we'd made in spreading the Gospel."

"And couldn't you see how that could be misconstrued?"

"No, John, I couldn't! I haven't admitted to anything so far that wasn't the truth. But let me tell you this, John Tindal— I'm sick and tired of being sick and tired and hungry and filthy! And I'll tell the colonel anything he wants to hear just so long as he doesn't send me back into that hellhole again!"

"Oh . . . Clare! How could you?" Tindal, said, his disappointment palpable.

"I'll tell you how, John!" she shouted, angry now. "I'm pregnant!"

Openmouthed, Tindal was taken by complete surprise. And so was Salehrad.

26

Fresh Intel

Konarak

The Northrop Grumman RQ-180 Stealth UAV surveillance drone was first deployed by the Air Force in 2015. Equipped with sensors far superior to earlier drones, it could fly higher and stay in the air longer, and was virtually invisible to radar. The units employed over Konarak were physically based out of Al Ahafra Air Base, just outside of Dubai, in the United Arab Emirates. They were controlled via satellite link, usually by a team of three, a qualified Air Force pilot, and two enlisted airmen, one to operate the sensors and electronic equipment, and another to operate the onboard ordnance. Since the drones employed over Konarak were unarmed (and therefore lighter, enabling them to stay over the target area longer), the team in Tempe, Arizona, controlling these units consisted of just two men: a pilot and an electronics specialist.

While the RQ-180 actually could fly at 60,000 feet, and the resolution of its cameras was excellent, they weren't really able to distinguish a dime on the ground from that height.

Its predecessor was the RQ-170, one of which had been downed in 2011 by an Iranian cyber warfare unit, which had hacked into its control signal and landed it. The RQ-180's electronic controls were far more secure and far less subject to being subverted by rogue enemy signals.

The drones deployed over Konarak were rotated every twenty-four hours. Since the trip from Al Ahafra to Konarak took just over two hours, the relief aircraft had to be airborne two hours in advance of the required rotation time. The Air Force had worked out a schedule for controlling the units by using five teams operating for four-hour shifts, with two of the teams overlapping while two drones were in the air simultaneously. The fact that Iran time was eleven-and-a-half hours earlier than Mountain Time only confused matters further.

It just so happened that a transition from one drone onsite to another was taking place just as the colonel, Clare Tindal, and a guard were boarding the Mercedes for the trip from the prison to the hotel. The vehicle's movement had been observed, but the number of passengers had not.

Further, the relief drone had not yet attained optimal altitude to observe the individual infrared heat signals of the passengers exiting the car at the hotel. It was at optimal altitude when only one person (the colonel) entered the vehicle for the return trip. It was logically assumed, therefore, that only one person had been in the car both ways, since only one person—designation "VIP"—had *ever* been previously observed traveling in the Mercedes, nothing whatever appeared to be out of order. And so it was, that moving Clare Tindal into the hotel had gone unobserved.

Observed that evening (Konarak time), and every evening thereafter, was that now *two* persons boarded the vehicle for the trip to the hotel, that *two* persons entered the hotel. But a short time later a single person left the hotel, boarded the vehicle, and drove it back to the prison. The Mercedes now remained parked outside the prison overnight, whereas, previously, the practice was to park it overnight at the hotel. The following morning, and every evening thereafter, one individual drove the vehicle to the hotel, and entered the hotel. A short time later, two people exited the hotel, boarded the vehicle, and drove to the prison. While what was being observed was actually the changing of the guard, the best explanation anyone in Tempe could come up with for this was that apparently the person (VIP) who used to drive the car himself now required a driver. Why a driver was now suddenly required to take the VIP to the hotel and escort him into the building was, however, a mystery.

Whether any of this was significant or not, escaped not only the drone operators, but also the SEAL team commanders in C2 at Little Creek.

Three days later, a trip from the prison to the hotel with three persons aboard the vehicle was noted, but since three persons returned two hours later, no alarm bells were rung. The total number of individuals onsite at the prison and at the hotel was apparently unchanged, after all. The team leader on that shift, an Air Force first lieutenant, did, however, make note of the unusual activity and report it to Little Creek.

All the very same information was subsequently passed on to Jake and his team aboard *Carolina,* as an EXODUS message via the regular 1400 radio transmission. Any significance of all the activity between the prison and the hotel in town escaped Jake, just as it had C2, and everyone else. As far as anyone on the Exodus team knew, all six of the prisoners were still onsite at Qajar prison.

That same evening, the president sent out this tweet:

@POTUS: If the cowardly Iranians won't let our people go, we'll go in after them. You don't mess with United States citizens!

27

Called on the Persian Carpet

Teheran

The president's tweet did not go unnoticed in the Iranian halls of power.

The Supreme Leader called the director of SAVAK in to the house of leadership for a rare audience. As always, Dariush, the Supreme Leader's personal secretary, sat well away from the conversation (but within earshot) and took notes.

"General," the Supreme Leader began, "you have seen the latest social media message from the President of the United States. What are we to make of it?"

"I suspect it is only more bluster from the man, Supreme Leader," the director answered. "Nonetheless, I think we are forced to take the threat seriously."

"So what is it that you recommend, General?"

"Well, Holiness, it is certainly entirely possible that the Americans could mount a special forces operation to rescue the American spies. But I am also entirely certain that the Americans do not know where the spies are being held. So it is difficult to see the point of mounting such an operation. Where would their generals send their soldiers exactly? How do you send in forces without knowing their destination?"

"That is not a recommendation, General," the Supreme Leader, annoyed, chided. "Get to the point."

"My apologies, Supreme Leader, I will try to be more brief." Still, the major general continued on with his train of thought. "As you know, Holiness, the network of American spies in Iran was disbanded with prejudice shortly after the Glorious Islamic Revolution. Sending in these six new spies can only be the evidence of a feeble attempt to reestablish an intelligence network in our country. I can only conclude that the Americans have no way of knowing that the Americans are not in Teheran, but elsewhere."

Now the Supreme Leader was beginning to worry. If the head of SAVAK took seriously the story that the six fool missionaries were actually spies . . .

The director droned on. "And that is why we have, so far, not placed guards outside the prison where the spies are being interrogated. We did this so as not to call attention to the SAVAK presence there. But now, in light of their president's bluster, I think it is only prudent that we take some reasonable precautions. I have ordered our man in Konarak, Colonel Salehrad, to mount a guard outside Qajar prison."

Finally, the man has come to the point, thought the Supreme Leader. "And do you think that simply mounting a guard outside the prison is a sufficient precaution?" he asked.

"I do, Holiness."

"Well I do not!" The general looked stunned at the Supreme Leader's angry outburst—and afraid. "I do not think you are taking the threat of an American special forces invasion seriously enough! Stop for a moment, and consider that the Americans *have* somehow found out exactly where the prisoners are being held. What would you do then?"

"Fortify the place?"

"Are you asking or recommending, General?" Still annoyed.

"Recommending, Holiness."

"Good. And I concur." Now the director looked relieved. "Still, we must also consider that the American president is not such a blustering fool after all, and that his message was simply a ploy to draw us out, make us take some action, deploy troops, do something to indicate where the prisoners are. Troop deployments can be observed, can they not? By spy drones and spy satellites?"

"Yes, Supreme Leader, unfortunately, yes they can."

"Very well then. Send a detachment of troops to Konarak to fortify Qajar prison. But also send detachments to Kashmar, Ahvaz, and Hamaden. And fortify the guard around SAVAK headquarters here in Teheran. "

"Immediately, Holiness. I will see to it right away."

But a platoon of regular army troops was not dispatched to Konarak or any of the other outlying locations before late in the following day, and the two transport trucks transporting the twenty-eight men to Konarak were still not en route until the morning of the next day.

28

Aboard *Roya*

Gulf of Oman

Hamid entered the hotel dining room for breakfast, and was a little surprised (and taken aback) when the colonel nodded to him as he passed by his table. *I hope he is just being polite,* he thought, *and has taken no special notice of me. Perhaps he has spies who reported I took Yasmina up to my room last night? No! I'm just being paranoid!*

The colonel finished first and, much to Hamid's relief, left the dining room without further acknowledging Hamid's presence. When Hamid mounted the bicycle for his trip to the docks, there was no sign of the colonel's Mercedes. The day was sunny overall, but there was a stiff breeze blowing, and puffs of grey clouds scudded across a hazy blue sky, even occasionally obscuring the sun. And it was also noticeably much cooler than it had been yesterday. En route, he passed by the drop point, and there was no chalk mark on the wall.

As he rode down the plank road that was the dock, Hamid noted that the waters of Chabahar Bay were nowhere near as calm as they had been the day before. The bay waters were choppy, with occasional wispy white caps. Amir was waiting for him aboard *Roya,* and had already stocked the boat with bait, ice, and lunch.

"Are you all right with this weather?" Amir asked. "The bay is unsettled, so the gulf is likely to be more unsettled still. If you suspect that you are not a good sailor, then perhaps we should stay in port until the weather clears. This is just a passing squall line, they come through here all the time. By late this afternoon, you will see, all will be calm again."

"No, Amir, I will be all right." Even as he said it, Hamid knew his comment was more bravado than reality. He was *not* a good sailor. Still, after his experience of the day before, he was unwilling to forego the chance of catching another big fish.

As *Roya* made her way into the gulf, Hamid thought better of his decision. In the gulf, the temperature had dropped further. The waters were *very* choppy, with blue-gray troughs perhaps a meter deep, the wind gusts forming white caps, the air wet, salty, and heavy. The sun was lost now behind grey cloud cover, and a line of rain, vertical strings of gray descending from the dark pillowed clouds above, could be seen off to the west.

And *Roya* was headed right for that squall line, rolling forward with a corkscrew motion. As a seemingly unconcerned and unaffected Amir stood placidly at the wheel, Hamid held on as long as he could. He willed himself to ignore the churning in his stomach, the roaring in his brain. That was until he leaned out over the side and lost his breakfast.

"We will turn back," Amir said. "Not everyone is a good sailor. There is no shame in that."

"I will be fine, now," Hamid said bravely. "Let us keep heading out."

Amir nodded, and against his better judgment, stayed on course. Hamid was, after all, the client.

159

Hamid concentrated at willing himself to feel better, but to no avail. He sat in the stern as Amir guided the boat westward, being thoroughly miserable. When *Roya* reached the squall line, after what seemed like hours to Hamid, he saw that the rain felt good on his face, and refused to get under the bridge shelter despite Amir's urging.

When the boat emerged on the other side of the squall line, the seas were much calmer, and Hamid was soaked through to the skin. But the sun was now peeping through the clouds again, and it was warmer than before. The sea was not much different than before, however, and the wind was still strong. And so *Roya* continued to pitch and roll. "Will we fish now?" Hamid asked Amir, trying hard to keep from his voice the misery he felt inside, and now outside as well.

"We can," Amir answered, "but trawling in this sea would be useless, I think. Perhaps we should just fish the reef?"

"Whatever you say, Amir, you are the guide."

Amir adjusted the wheel and headed the boat in a new direction. On this course, *Roya's* motion was not so upsetting. After some time had passed, he announced, "Here is a good place." How Amir knew that this spot in the gulf was any different from any other spot was mystifying to Hamid. They were out of sight of land, and with nothing other than a glimpse of sun, a compass, and his watch to go by, how Amir knew that this place was a "good place" could be nothing short of witchery.

Amir headed the boat into the oncoming sea, and ran it forward at dead slow. This now minimized the boat's motion, which Hamid greatly appreciated, although by now he was gaining some sea legs. Amir dropped four baited lines over the side and said, "You tend these two. When you feel the line hit bottom, reel the line in until you are a meter or so off the bottom."

Hamid tried to follow those instructions, but *Roya's* surging motion made judging the distance of the hook from the bottom near impossible. Still, he got a bite on both his lines almost immediately, as did Amir. Each pole had about eighteen meters of line out, and hauling the catch up was real work, especially with a hooked fish fighting all the way to the surface.

The two men hauled up catch after catch. They caught redfish mostly, but grouper, bream and grunts as well. Amir kept only the larger fish, gently unhooking and returning to the sea anything under two hundred millimeters (about eight inches) or so. Still, in just over an hour, the fish box was full, and the two men had caught about fifty good-sized fish. And by this time, in the now full sun, Hamid's clothing had almost completely dried out.

"The box is full," Amir announced. "If we catch any more fish we must throw them back!"

"And I am tired," Hamid agreed. "Let us head in for the day."

"But it is early yet. We have not even had lunch!"

"*You* can eat on the way in," Hamid replied. "The fish box is full, and you have more than earned your pay."

The squall line had preceded them to the east, and the seas were now much calmer, and *Roya's* bouncing about had pretty much ceased. Reluctantly, Amir turned *Roya* about and headed back toward the mouth of the bay.

* * * * *

"What was it like in the seventies, Amir?" Amir had finished his lunch, and Hamid asked the question as they headed in. "Was the economy any better then?"

"No," he answered. "No better, but different. And I was a firebrand back then. I had just converted to Islam, and was convinced that a rededication of our country to the true religion was the answer to all our ills. I was convinced that the shah had been corrupted by foreigners—the British and the Americans."

"You said you are a convert to the faith. What were you before?"

"Pretty much nothing. My parents were Maronite Christians, and we even had a Maronite church in Konarak—Saint Joseph's—it is a museum now. The shah's government was tolerant of the People of the Book back then, both Christians and Jews. My parents tried to raise me as a Christian, but it never took, not even when I was little." He paused, as if in reflection. "Then," Amir continued, "when the shah declared himself an emperor, even as the economy was in shambles, the common people took to the streets. And by the common people, I mean the Muslims. I wanted to be part of it, and so I embraced Islam. And that is the story of my conversion. Not much of a story, is it?"

"We all have our reasons for doing the things we do. Your deep discontent was certainly reason enough."

"Was it? Now we have an Islamic Republic, and the economy is still shitty."

"Your parents?"

"Long dead. When they shuttered their church and deported the priest to Syria, my parents and the other

Christians were 'encouraged' to embrace Islam. Some refused, and disappeared. My parents and some others feigned conversion, but continued worshipping as Christians in secret. I thought seriously about reporting them to the police — remember I was still a firebrand at the time — but finally thought better of it. In the Quran, after all, the Prophet makes special allowance for People of the Book."

"He does," Hamid agreed. After that, both men maintained a reflective silence as *Roya* entered the bay and made for the marina.

At dockside, with *Roya* tied up, Amir asked Hamid, "What will you do with your fish?"

"What?" he answered. "The fish? What could I possibly do with them? You take them."

Amir grinned his yellow, broken-tooth grin. "You know these fish are valuable, and you are sure you want me to take them?"

"Amir, you know full well I can't take the fish."

"Very well, but there is still the matter of the day's rental."

Now amused, Hamid paid Amir the fee that they had agreed upon the previous day. "Here you are," he said, handing him a small wad of euros, "but you know you are a thief, right?"

"Perhaps," Amir agreed, "but an honest one. Why do you not pick a fish or two out of the box and I will filet them. Take them to any good restaurant in town and they will prepare them for you."

"Now that," Hamid said, "is an excellent idea." He thought of his dinner date with Yasmina set for that evening.

"Will you be going out again tomorrow?" Amir asked, interrupting his thoughts. "If I get a good price for these fish, I can afford to lower my fee somewhat. "

"Well," Hamid observed, "I *am* here for the fishing. I will meet you in the morning, same time."

* * * * *

Hamid rode the bicycle back toward the hotel carrying a package of four, nice-sized redfish filets. When he rode past the drop box there was a chalk mark on the wall.

He parked the bike and sat on the bench. He sat a while and observed. The street was empty. After ten minutes, only one elderly woman had passed by, and the street was once again empty. He found and palmed the thumb drive, and waited some more. Again, no one. He got up, finally, and, as furtively as he could, rubbed off the chalk mark. He then got back on the bicycle, and rode back to the hotel.

The thumb drive bore the directive: "Extraction set for tonight. Keep cell phone charged and on. You will be notified if needed."

Shit! He thought, *Now I'll have to figure out a way to dump Yasmina! That's what happens whenever I start to think with my balls!*

And he was disappointed that now he and Yasmina could not share the fillets he carried. He was really looking forward to dinner and what was sure to follow.

29

Leaving *Carolina* Behind

Sea of Oman

Commander Helfenstein managed to maneuver *Carolina* within five klicks (2.7 nautical miles) of the beach, bringing Jake and his team five klicks closer than originally planned. It was 1930 local time and the sun had set thirty-two minutes earlier.

Carolina was brought up to what in the old diesel boats would have been periscope depth, for *Carolina,* a keel depth of 104 feet. Unlike the old boats, depth control was fly-by-wire, and did not require the attention of a diving officer; the petty officer operating a control console simply dialed in the desired depth, and a computer took it from there. Once on station, *Carolina's* photonics mast was raised, and a complete surface search, visual and electronic, was conducted. Only when no contacts were found was word sent down to the missile room to "commence lockout procedure, port and starboard trunks."

Jake, Fowles, Bonsignore, and their equipment were already inside the starboard lockout trunk, while Cole, Wilson, Janelli, their equipment, and the inflatable were in the port trunk. The men wore wetsuits, with masks, snorkels, and flashlights handy. Each breathed filtered ship's air through hand-held, soft, silicone masks that covered just mouth and nose. No swim fins or SCUBA gear were worn because the team would be in the water only long enough to exit the sub, free rise to the surface, and deploy the inflatable. The bends was also not an issue, as the men would not be under pressure long enough for nitrogen to dissolve into their blood.

When the order was received, and under the watchful eye of the COB, the lower trunk doors were shut and secured, and the sea cocks opened, allowing seawater to enter the chambers. Watertight lights inside the chambers were more about making the men inside comfortable and providing a sense of security, since they provided minimal illumination. As the chambers filled, the pressure inside the trunks rose, and would continue to rise, until equalized with sea pressure outside the submarine.

The pressure regulators on each man's breathing apparatus adjusted the pressure of the air breathed as the sea pressure increased. The air pressure in each man's lungs was thus equalized to that being exerted on his body. As the pressure increased, each man avoided rupturing his ear drums by pressing his nostrils closed, and blowing hard against his Eustachian tubes, thus equalizing the pressure in the middle ear.

Only when the pressure inside the trunk was equal to that of the water outside could the upper hatch be opened. When gauges inside the missile room indicated that the pressures were equalized, the COB saw that it was now safe to open the upper hatches. As each upper hatch was cracked, the remaining air inside the lockout trunks escaped, seawater flooding in to fill the void. Finally, both hatches were opened wide.

The inflatable was then released from the port tube and, buoyant, it shot to the surface, where it partially deployed as the air trapped inside it expanded. Still inside the lockout trunks, each man took a full, deep breath and discarded his breathing apparatus. Each man quickly donned his diving mask, and, in a practiced maneuver, cleared it of trapped water by pressing the upper part of the mask to the forehead with the palm of the hand, and breathing out into the mask, forcing the water inside the mask out through the bottom seal. Then, masks dry, each one let go of his handhold on the trunk wall and began the free rise over the sixty-two feet to the surface, not swimming, just gently kicking his legs, towing his gear behind, and forcefully exhaling as he rose.

Surfacing from any depth of water can be very dangerous. When breathing compressed air at depth, its pressure must be regulated to match the pressure of the air to the pressure of the surrounding water. That way, the air in one's lungs matches the water pressure outside. This is the case with air delivered by SCUBA gear or the ship-supplied air breathed by Jake and his team in the escape trunk.

Observing the bubbles released by a scuba diver from any depth, the observer will note that the bubbles grow ever larger as they rise. The same thing would happen to the compressed air inside a person's lungs, if, abandoning their scuba gear (or leaving an escape trunk air supply), they rose to the surface holding their breath. The air inside one's lungs would expand as the person rose, until their lungs exploded. It would, in short, cause an air embolism.

In leaving the lockout trunks, then, it was imperative that the men exiting Carolina *continuously breathe out, forcing the air out of their lungs as they rise. Anyone who has ever performed this maneuver (called a "free rise") is surprised that, as they rise, there is still plenty of air remaining to be forced out of one's lungs. Indeed, if at any time they feel comfortable, then they are in big trouble.*

On the surface, the sea was the color of liquid slate, dead calm, with not so much as a gentle ripple. A quarter moon was just above the western horizon, darkened only by wispy clouds pushed lazily along by an upper warm, wet, and gentle offshore breeze.

Cole used the supplied compressed air bottle to completely inflate the rubber boat. Each man then entered the boat, and then bailed out the water he inevitably brought into the boat with him. Finally, the equipment bags were brought aboard. Jake and Cole opened their bags and took out their M4a1s. Jake and Cole stood guard as the rest of the team paddled, heading the inflatable in toward the beach.

Just over a half-hour after arriving on station, and having observed the SEAL team's progress with the photonics system, *Carolina* lowered the photonics mast and cleared the area.

The visibility was much better than Jake would have preferred — about fifteen klicks. There were some shore lights visible from seaward, and a glow off on the horizon, which was most likely from the Konarak city lights. And there were also, thankfully, no patrol boats.

On the beach, the perimeter road that was shown on Jake's map stretched west to east along the shoreline, a black asphalt ribbon set well above the highwater mark. Further off in the distance, and also paralleling the shoreline, a light gray band jutting up from the beach marked the cliffs that must somehow be scaled if the team was to reach the prison. There was practically no cover on the beach itself, so the team members knew they must move as fast as they were able, if they were to have any chance of avoiding discovery. They dragged the inflatable and their packs across the sand up to, and over, the perimeter road. They could, they found, at least find some cover in the depression between the beach and the roadway beyond and the perimeter road. There the road surface stood about level with their knees when they stood upright.

They had been lucky thus far, and there had been no traffic on the road, but now, off to the west, the loom of headlights appeared, and a vehicle approached. Cole and Fowles quickly flipped open the vent valves on the boat, so that at least it had started to deflate before the oncoming vehicle was on top of them. After that, there was nothing for it but for the team to lie flat on the ground beside the roadway until the vehicle passed. Which it eventually did, without incident.

Jake found the radiotelephones and gave two to Cole, taking one for himself. Then he established contact with C2 in Virginia Beach, as the men began digging a hole in the sand using their paddles.

"Exodus Base, this is Exodus Alfa, do you read, over?"

"This is Exodus Base, read you five by five, Alfa, over." Jake recognized the voice, even over the radiotelephone: Clegg.

"Roger that, Base. 'The eagle has landed,' over."

"This is Base. The terrain just *looks* like that of the moon, Alfa. What is your location, over?"

"Just north of perimeter road, about a klick west of the north-south roadway, over."

"Roger that. Note that security has increased at your objective. There is now one guard at the door and two perimeter guards, over."

"Alfa understands that objective now has three outside guards posted, one at door, two on perimeter. Anything else, Base? Over."

"Negative Alfa. Just be careful. Base, out."

"Hear that, men?" Jake said. "They got smart and posted outside guards."

"So we heard, L-T," Cole noted, "so we heard," and the other four men nodded, still digging.

By the time they had removed their wet suits, changed into their flak shirts and desert fatigues, and buried all their seagoing gear inside the deflated boat, it was 2050. By 2105, they had donned battle gear. But there was a problem. The night vision gear was supposed to attach to their helmets. And it fit on the regular-issue helmets just fine. But with the fancy new helmets they had just been issued, they were enough bigger than standard issue so that there was no way to attach the apparatus.

"Not to worry," Jerry Bonsignore, said, and produced a roll of duct tape from his pack. "One size fits all," he said, and jury-rigged the night vision gear and attached it to each man's helmet. Janelli, in turn, attached Bonsignore's gear. The arrangement looked very "Mickey Mouse," but it worked. And now they were finally outfitted for action.

They then trekked east along the perimeter road until they reached the north-south main road. Jake had been right; it was just a kilometer away. Turning north along the main road, they began their journey toward the looming Konarak City lights in the distance. From here on, the path led up over the cliffs and onward to Qajar prison.

30

The Situation Room

Washington, D.C.

The secretary of state was conspicuous by his absence. The president was there, as was the vice president and the secretaries of defense, and of the navy. Also, there was the president's national security advisor, and the director of the CIA, along with the chairman of the joint chiefs, and V.Adm. Williams, who was in charge of Navy special operations. All sat in rapt attention, staring at the sixty-inch plasma screen on one wall of the situation room in the basement of the White House. Representative Longstreet had begged the president to let him join them in the situation room, but the president had ruled against it. "You're too close to this, Bob," he had said, "Better you stay away and let the professionals do their job." Longstreet was unhappy about it, but he couldn't argue with the president's logic.

The plasma screen showed a live feed from the RQ-180 stealth drone flying high over the city of Konarak, in the Islamic Republic of Iran. It was 7:30 AM in Washington, D.C.

A Navy SEAL team, just six men, were on the ground in Iran, six red dots on the infra-red feed. And communications between the Command and Control Center in Virginia, with both the men on the ground and the drone controller in Arizona, were being piped in. Williams was briefing the president as the situation on the ground unfolded.

"Virginia has just informed the people on the ground that, for some reason, the Iranians have increased security around the prison where our people are being held. Before, there were no guards outside the prison. Now, for whatever reason, they've posted a perimeter guard and a guard outside the only entrance." But he was thinking, *Yeah, and they did that because you, Sir, had to boast to the world on Twitter that we were coming in after our people.*

"Okay," the president answered, "How come there's a time delay in these transmissions?"

"That's because, Sir, the signals are being bounced off a communications satellite, and it takes time for the signals to make the circuit."

"Yeah, okay. Right. I see that. And it's really annoying."

31

Other Situations

Konarak

Hamid, carrying the redfish filets Amir had prepared, arrived at the place where he and Yasmina had arranged to meet. He was surprised to see her waiting there dressed as when he first met her, in what she had termed her "frumpy" clothes. And she was in tears.

"Yasmina, what is the matter?" he asked, and observed, "You are still dressed for work."

"I have not been home as yet," she said, still sobbing.

"Because . . ." he prompted.

"Because Taraneh went to my home last night and spoke to my parents while we were at dinner. She told them that I had flirted with you on the road into town, and that you were obviously up to no good. She said that she was concerned for my virtue, but the *jinn* only did it because she is jealous and vindictive."

"And so, what happened? What did your parents do?"

"What do you think they did? They checked on my room, and, of course, I was not there, because I was with you.

"My father beat me. He beat me on my ass with a leather strap," she sobbed, "He called me a slut and a whore. And, even worse, he told me that as soon as this job was done, he and my mother were arranging a marriage for me with Jawed, the eldest son of the fisherman Raman, and . . ." Yasmina was crying so hard by then, that she had to stop and catch her breath. "And Jawed is an ugly pig! And if you don't take me with you to Teheran, I will be stuck in this shitty godforsaken hellhole forever!"

Hamid made to hold her, so as to comfort her, but Yasmina pulled away. "I have to go home, now. I am already late. My father will probably beat me again for being late." She turned from him and ran away.

* * * * *

Hamid rode the bicycle back to the hotel. *Well,* he consoled himself, *at least now I don't have to scheme my way out of having dinner with Yasmina.*

He had the hotel restaurant prepare the redfish fillets for his dinner. After what was a really excellent meal (but no substitute for another romp with Yasmina), he went up to his second-floor suite and retired early. It had been a very tiring day, after all. Following his latest instructions, he had, until then, kept his secure cell phone turned on, and on vibrate. Now he put it on ringtone as well, and placed it on charge on the nightstand next to the bed. He had always been a light sleeper, and he knew that if it rang, it would awaken him.

* * * * *

Back in his room at the hotel in Konarak, Colonel Salehrad was nursing a Beefeater gin and tonic and rereading *Great Expectations*, relaxing before bed. He loved Dickens, and he had read everything the man ever wrote at least once. An adjoining door separated his suite from the room next door, where Clare Tindal slept. There was, he knew, a guard in the hallway, just outside the entry door to her room. The man was his man, SAVAK, and would remain alert for his entire twelve-hour shift. He would never dare to do otherwise.

* * * * *

In her room, Clare Tindal slept fitfully. She should have been comfortable and sleeping soundly, once more in a real bed, and not lying on a concrete floor. But devils haunted her dreams: Screwtape and Wormwood.

32

In Country

Konarak

The main road up to the town from the beach provided even less cover than the perimeter road. There was a shallow drainage ditch on the east side of the road. The plan was, if a car passed, to lie flat in the ditch and hope that they wouldn't be noticed. It was not much of a plan, of course, but there wasn't much else that could be done.

Everything was good, and the team had advanced almost a klick up the road when a vehicle coming down the perimeter road turned up onto the main thoroughfare. As the headlights swept up from the south, the six men dived into the ditch. Luckily, it hadn't rained in some time, and the ditch was, at least, dry.

Something was strange. The vehicle's headlights kept sweeping back and forth across the road. As the vehicle, a light pickup truck, passed them, Jake could see why. The truck was weaving all over the road, and the driver was obviously impaired. A short distance up the road from where the team lay hidden, the truck stopped. It was on an angle from the center of the road, the right front wheel off the roadway and almost in the ditch. The driver left the vehicle, staggered around the front of the truck, and, bathed in the beam of the headlights, proceeded to urinate into the ditch up ahead.

Suddenly, the whole scene was alight. Another vehicle, heading south, was now passing the parked truck. The driver honked his horn, and he and his passengers were shouting derisively at the truck driver as they passed. That car proceeded south, toward the perimeter road. And its occupants apparently had taken no notice of the SEALs. The truck driver, startled by the passing car, and still holding himself, had spun around, and fallen backward into the ditch.

When Jake and the others reached him, he was unconscious, pants open, and face up in a drunken stupor.

"What do we do?" Wilson asked, his question addressed to nobody in particular.

"Waddya mean, 'What do we do?' " Cole replied. "We ride!"

Riding north in the bed of the beat-up old Toyota Tacoma, Wilson asked Fowles (who, after all, had served *two* tours in Afghanistan, spoke Pushto, and was therefore the authority on all things Islamic), "How come that guy was drunk? I thought it was against their religion for Muslims to drink alcohol."

"It is, strictly forbidden by Sharia law," Fowles answered. He had studied the subject. "And, here in Iran, it's also against civil law. Punishable by seventy-four lashes, man or woman alike. But apparently that doesn't seem to stop anybody."

"Guess not," Wilson agreed.

The Toyota proceeded north, following the road up over the cliffs and onto the plateau, the truck headlights off. The glow from the night lights of Konarak now lit up the northeastern sky. Looking at the map, Jake had Cole pull the truck off the road and stop about half a klick from the prison. It was 2157.

"Okay, gents, it's on foot from here," Jake said. "Activate your night vision gear. We need to reconnoiter and get the lay of the land. I need to know how many guards there really are outside, and where they are. Then we fall back and figure out how we take them out. Fowles and Bonsignore, you're with the Chief. Wilson and Janelli, with me. Meet back here at 2230. Questions?" None. "Okay, Let's head out."

As they approached the prison, they heard the music, a discordant wailing, growing ever louder the closer they advanced.

Qajar prison was dimly lit. Some light showed from the ground floor windows, and none showed from the second floor. There was a light fixture above the only entry door, but it was not lit. A guard was clearly visible there, however, in the green glow of the night vision gear. The Mercedes was parked in front of and along the building at the east end. The perimeter guards were harder to spot. They were dug in at opposite ends of the prison, giving each emplacement a field of fire from the front to the back of the structure from either end. There was one man in each gun emplacement. The door guard carried a rifle. There was no telling how the perimeter guards were armed, but Jake guessed that there was at least a light machine gun in each dugout.

They checked all around the outside of the building, and there were no other outside guards, just the three that Exodus Base had described. Recon complete, the SEALs retired toward the truck.

On the way back to the truck, Jake felt the satellite phone vibrate. C2 wanted a report, but wouldn't be alarmed if nobody reported in; C2 knew Jake would report in a soon as it was safe to do so. Cole carried two similar phones, both turned off. Had they also been on, they still would not have been answered under any circumstances, unless it was safe to do so.

Back at the Toyota, Jake did report in. "Exodus Base, this is Exodus Alfa. Over."

"This is Base, Alfa. What is your situation? Over."

"We have arrived just outside of objective, have done a recon, and are now preparing to secure the place. Over."

"Roger that. We'll let you get on with it. Keep us informed. Base, out."

Then the team compared notes and set about planning their attack.

"What in hell was that racket?" Cole asked. "Sounded like a hundred cats being shaken in a burlap bag."

"If we can hear it outside the prison, think how loud it must be inside," Jake observed. "I'm guessing it's just another way of torturing the prisoners."

"Torture is right," Cole agreed.

Jake then returned to solving the problems at hand. "We need to take the guards out quietly, if at all possible. But if there's no other choice, and it's them or you, make sure it's them. Don't hesitate to use your weapon, " Jake cautioned. "Okay. We'll take the perimeter posts out first. Quietly. When they're both taken out, we do the guard at the door."

The men nodded.

"Good. Chief?"

"Two teams each on the gun emplacements," Cole said. "Fowles, and Bonsignore, on the east one, and Wilson, and Janelli, on the west. Approach on your bellies from the rear. Not much cover, just some low scrub, so you use the land contours just like we've trained. Move low, slow, and careful-like. You guys take 'em out—quietly—and the L-T and I will

179

cover you. When the perimeters are secured, the L-T and I will end-around to the corners of the building, L-T to the west, me to the east. I'll set up behind the Mercedes, the L-T draws the guard's attention, while I sidle up and take him out. Questions?"

"Yeah, Chief," Bonsignore said. "How come you get to take out the guard on the door? I'm faster."

"True that," Cole answered. "But *I'm* the Chief."

Still snickering, Jake said, "It's 2240. Chances are, if there's a change of guard, it'll be at midnight. So let's take these guys out before then, if we can. Be damn careful. Good hunting."

33

Inside Qajar

Konarak

The man the prisoners called Screwtape was restless. He knew he should try to sleep, but had tossed and turned in his bunk since turning off the satellite TV downstairs, and joining the three men already asleep in the upstairs barracks. As the senior enlisted man in the barracks, he had not drawn guard duty. But ever since the colonel had set up the three outside guard posts, and his partner (the man the prisoners called Wormwood) had been pressed into guard duty, he had to carry the load of interrogating the prisoners by himself. Not that he didn't love his work, mind you, but it was exhausting, and now he couldn't sleep. He had managed to doze off earlier, but had awaken with an erection. *Why should the prisoners be allowed to sleep when I cannot?*

Not that he could imagine how they managed to sleep with all with those bright lights and that awful racket! Despite the ear plugs that he and the other three men in the room were wearing, he could still hear that infernal *al-Balochi* music, just not nearly as loud. Of course, there was nothing in his orders that said he couldn't disturb the prisoners' sleep, should circumstances dictate. In fact, the colonel had frequently scheduled middle-of-the-night interrogations. And the colonel *had* said that the woman called Mary Rogers was still fair game. He got up from the bed and pulled on his trousers.

In the basement, despite the ear plugs, the wailing from the overhead speakers was overwhelming. Screwtape peered into the cages. The three men were sprawled on the floor of their cage asleep—a fitful sleep, perhaps, but sleep nonetheless. He then unlocked the women's cage, grabbed a sleeping Mary Rogers by her upper arm, and dragged her to the cage door. Startled and suddenly awake, she saw it was Screwtape who had grabbed her. Without sufficient energy to scream, she could only whimper. Adele Crowley moaned and turned, but never woke. Neither did any of the three weak and exhausted men in the adjoining cell.

Screwtape didn't bother with the handcuffs or the blackout hood. He frog-walked Mary Rogers directly to the interrogation room, his whole body tingling in anticipation.

34

Breaking and Entering

Konarak

Fowles and Bonsignore leapfrogged toward their target in the east gun emplacement, one covering the other as they took turns advancing, crawling on their bellies, taking advantage of whatever meager cover the uneven terrain provided.

Emanating from the prison, the wailing of the discordant music droned on.

The guard stood in the dugout, waist high, facing the prison building, a rifle slung over his shoulder. A machine gun was emplaced on a parapet, and was aimed toward the building. For whatever reason, the guard turned toward the approaching men, peering out into the dark. Bonsignore, the man closest to him, froze motionless, face down in the sand. Fowles, about ten yards behind Bonsignore, crouched low, his M4a1 at the ready. The guard unslung his own rifle, stepped out of the dugout, and headed straight toward Bonsignore. The guard was unzipping his fly as he walked, obviously looking for a spot, well away from his post, to relieve himself. Three more paces and he would be on top of Bonsignore.

Sensing, rather than seeing, the man's presence, Bonsignore jumped up, and in one smooth motion, drew his Ka-bar from its sheath, and sliced open the man's throat. But as the guard fell, he reflexively depressed the trigger on his rifle. The distinctive ragged *Brapt! Brapt! Brapt!* sound of a Kalashnikov broke the night silence three times, as three rounds split the damp air before the man's body hit the ground.

The guard manning the west dugout, hearing the shots over the din from inside the building, shouted out an alarm, and aimed his machine gun toward their source. But less than a second later, Wilson struck him from behind. And Wormwood died silently.

The guard at the door had unslung his rifle in response to the commotion, and stood at the ready, searching, should anyone approach the prison entrance. Cole saw that getting close enough to take the man out quietly was out of the question. And, since the shots already fired were sure to alert the other men inside the building, he aimed and fired his M4a1. *Brrrp, Brrrp, Brrrp!* The three rounds Cole expertly tapped out killed the man where he stood.

The six SEALs were together at the door seconds later. Bonsignore arrived first. "Told you I was faster," he whispered to Cole, who only scowled in return. They could hear, now louder still, that weird loud music coming from inside the building.

Surely the men inside would be at the ready and waiting as soon as the door was opened. Jake, Fowles and Bonsignore stood to one side, with Wilson and Janelli standing opposite, all with their weapons at the ready. Cole stomped the door open, quickly ducking to one side so as to avoid the hail of bullets that was sure to follow.

But there were no bullets. There was nobody there.

Nobody was waiting for them.

The SEALs, absorbing their surprise, and not questioning their good luck, followed their training, and, filing inside, began clearing the premises. They noticed first off that all the racket was emanating from the basement: the wailing singing, and, to Western ears, the discordant accompaniment. The first floor layout was just as had been described, except that the stairwell was more centrally located, and not against the east wall. Ignoring the noise, they quietly searched the first floor and found no one.

Jake signaled to Cole that he was to take Fowles and Bonsignore, and clear the top floor while he attended to the basement with the others.

When Cole and his team entered the top floor barracks room, they found three men fast asleep, each man wearing ear plugs against the noise emanating from the basement. *That explains why they never heard the shots fired outside,* Cole thought, *and while nobody was waiting for us at the front door.*

Leaving Fowles to watch the sleepers, Cole signaled to Bonsignore to watch his back as he set about clearing the private bedroom. It was empty. The sleepers, still covered by Fowles, were awakened one by one, each in turn having his wrists bound by zip ties to their beds. Bonsignore produced the roll of duct tape from his pack and improvised gags for each man. For good measure, he also zip tied each man's ankles together.

"Consider yourselves, lucky," Bonsignore said in his fluent Russian, as he attended to each of the three men. "Our orders said not to waste any of you unless it could not be avoided. Well, with those poor bastards outside, it could not be avoided." The men, uncomprehending, gazed up at Bonsignore wide-eyed, and in fear for their lives.

185

Jake led his team into the basement. The din from the loudspeakers could have awakened the dead. But the stench of the place was enough to send the dead back to the refuge of their graves. In the large room with the cages, he found four of the prisoners confined, three men and one woman, sound asleep on the floor. He left it to Wilson to open the cages and get those four ready to travel. He also gave him the mission of silencing the din. With Janelli, he went in search of the missing two missionaries. They found the first two rooms to the east empty. When they opened the third room, Jake almost got sick to his stomach.

35

Clare's Room

Konarak

Clare Tindal awoke in her bed and immediately felt that something was very wrong. There was a sticky wetness between her legs. She knew exactly what it was, and began to cry softly. *I'm having my period!*

She rose from the bed, went into the bathroom and cleaned herself. Folding a washcloth in three, she improvised a sanitary napkin, positioning the washcloth inside her granny panties and pulled them up in place under her nightgown. Then she sat down on the divan that was set against the wall opposite the foot of her bed—*and* she stopped crying. Instead, she seethed in anger. And all of her anger was directed at the colonel. It was *he* that had abducted her and her companions off the street, it was *he* who had moved them all to that hellhole of a prison, and it was *he*—despite his contentions to the contrary—it was *he* who had orchestrated the torture, the rape, the starvation.

It was the colonel's ministrations that were responsible for her period being late, that had fooled her into thinking that, *finally*, she would bear a child. And it was the colonel that had convinced her to betray her friends, her husband, her *country*, all for the sake of a child that never was, and that might never, ever, be.

Clare Tindal seethed. *It's the Colonel who is responsible for all this evil, every last bit of it. And, now, God forgive me, with all of my being, I hate him. Please, Lord, make* me *the instrument of your justice!*

36

The Situation Room

Washington, D.C.

"What's happening? What's going on there?" the president asked. He addressed the question to anyone in the situation room who might give him an answer.

"We're not sure, Mr. President, " V.Adm. Williams replied. "You've seen and heard exactly what we have. Our people on the ground—the SEALs—were okay when they entered the prison. They appear to have dispatched the three men standing guard outside without much trouble. But once they went inside, we're not sure what they ran into, and they haven't reported in yet. My guess is that they've been a bit too busy to do so. It's only been a few minutes, though. Give them a chance. We'll just have to let my SEALs do what they do best. Till then, we wait."

"But what about the missionaries? The evangelicals—are they all right?"

When no one else volunteered, the Williams again spoke up. "Well," he replied, "neither has the SEAL team asked C2 to scramble the helicopters. They'll do that when they've accounted for the prisoners."

"So we *don't* know if the missionaries are all right!"

"Please, Mr. President," Helen Siebert pleaded, "our men on the ground are the best in the world. We must be patient, and give them a chance to do their job. They have to clear that whole prison, room by room. That takes time. Please be patient."

The President scowled. Patience was not his long suit.

37

Qajar Prison

Konarak

The man the prisoners called Screwtape was stripped to the waist, and in his hand he held a flexible plastic rod. The woman was suspended by her wrists from overhead, naked, her inner thighs bloody, her body covered with angry red welts, raw and bleeding. Screwtape was poised, arm held out wide and away from his body, to deliver yet another blow.

The cacophony suddenly stopped. Jake had heard shots fired from the direction of room with the cages. Slewfoot Wilson, he surmised, had used his weapon to shoot out, and silence, the overhead speakers. *Thank you, Slew,* he thought, *and now to deal with this bastard.*

The ear plugs he wore had only diminished the noise, and Screwtape knew immediately that the wailing and undulating rhythms had been silenced. He looked up from his work and turned to the doorway, where he saw Jake, standing there in full battle gear. And he saw another soldier similarly garbed just behind him, in the hallway. Without thinking, Screwtape, wielding the thin rod, ran to attack the two intruders. Without hesitation, Jake raised his M4a1 and dropped the man in his tracks.

The woman, once released, collapsed on the floor beneath her. Jake found the filthy prison garment she had worn, and decided that helping her back into it might do more harm than good. Sure, it would cover her nakedness, but, with all her open cuts, might also cause some serious infections. Instead, he sent Janelli back upstairs to look for a blanket, or something else, to cover her.

Finding nothing appropriate on the ground floor, Janelli shouted up to Bonsignore on the second floor, asking if it had been cleared. When Bonsignore answered in the affirmative, he took the stairs two-by-two, stripped a blanket off one of the bunks, and quickly returned to Jake and Mary Rogers in the basement torture chamber, where he found that Wilson had joined Jake, and was cleaning up Mary Rogers as best he could. Wilson and Jake helped her stand, wrapped her in the blanket Janelli had brought, and, Janelli following, helped her up the stairs to the ground floor, where the other SEALs and the other four prisoners from the cages were waiting. Bonsignore had found some bottled water, and was cautioning the other four missionaries to "Just sip it, slowly."

* * * * *

"You have to go after Clare, my wife, Clare—Clare Tindal—Captain," John Tindal pleaded.

"Lieutenant," Jake corrected, and then realized how lame that was—insisting this civilian use his correct rank—given the situation. "Where is she? Do you have any idea where she is?"

"She's in town," Tindal said. "She's in a hotel in town."

And Jake thought *I probably know just which hotel that is.*

"Okay," Jake said, "even if we find this hotel, Mr. Tindal, we would have to tear the whole place apart to find her. By the time we do that, we'll have the entire Iranian Army all over us. I'm truly sorry, but we don't have the time. If we don't get the five of you that we *do* have out, and out quick, then *none* of us will get out."

"But I know exactly which room she's in. If you can get me to the hotel, I can take you straight to her room. Third floor, turn right, next to the last door on the left! I've been there!"

"Would you recognize the hotel from the outside if you saw it?" Jake asked.

"I would! I would! Lieutenant, I tell you I've *been* there!"

Jake got on the satellite radio and reported in to C2. He quickly apprised Porter and Clegg of the situation on the ground: Five of the six missionaries were secured; it was Clare Tindal that was missing; and that her husband could, and was willing, to guide him to her location in town. One of the regular guards who should have been there at the prison was not, so was probably with Mrs. Tindal, along with the VIP, in town. "Wait one," came the initial response, and so he impatiently awaited C2's instructions.

Instead, he got questions.

"This is Base. If you think you could pull it off, how long do you think this little side excursion to the hotel will take you, Alfa? Over." Again, even over the satellite radio, Jake recognized Clegg's raspy voice.

"It all depends, Base, on the choppers' ETA, over." He glanced at his watch. It was 2317.

"This is Base. The carrier is a hundred miles offshore. Once we notify the carrier, and the choppers are scrambled, the choppers will be onsite in just over one half-hour. It is not advisable for choppers to stay onsite for more than one half-hour, so you would have just over one hour—call it six-three minutes—to get to the missing package, and return to evac point in time. Doubt seriously you could pull that off, Alfa. Over."

"Do you have an estimated travel time to package location? Over."

"If package location is same as VIP, which is by no means certain, and you have use of a vehicle, then approximately ten minutes. But it's still too risky. Base cannot authorize your jeopardizing one package already secured to retrieve the lost package, over."

"Understood. But assuming lost package location is same as VIP location, and package spouse can verify on arrival, that gives Alfa four-zero minutes onsite to retrieve lost package. If she's not at VIP location, we turn around and come back to the evac point, and nothing is lost. Believe that is doable, Base. I say again, *can do*. Is Base able to vector Alfa to VIP location? Over."

"Forget it, Alfa. Base cannot, I say again, *cannot* authorize lost package retrieval. Over."

"Come back, Base?" Jake clicked the "Send" button on his phone a few times. "Exodus Base, this is Exodus Alfa. You're cutting out. Over."

"Cut the crap, Jake, I'm scrambling those choppers — *Now!* Clegg was pissed enough to break radio protocol. In response, and to maintain the ruse (despite Clegg having seen right through it), Jake switched off the phone.

Jake was by no means sure that he could pull off Clare Tindal's rescue, and was even less sure it was worth risking John Tindal's life in the process. The smart move would be to go with the bird in the hand, follow orders, rescue the five "packages" the SEALs had already retrieved, and call it a day. Mission complete, if not completely accomplished.

But Jake turned the radiotelephone back on and transmitted: "This is Exodus Alfa. Exodus Alfa acknowledges Exodus Base's permission to proceed with lost package retrieval. Out." Then he switched the phone off again.

Of course, there had been no such permission, but Jake wanted his superiors to know that he was about to disobey orders. He knew very well that Porter and Clegg would now be pissed off beyond belief. And, he knew that there would be hell to pay if, and when, he ever got home. But he also knew that they would now do everything in their power to ensure that his little planned side excursion was a success.

* * * * *

Back in the situation room, the president was nervous, but pleased. C2 had informed V.Adm. Williams that the command lieutenant on the ground at Konarak was going to take the risk of going into town to rescue the missing missionary, and Williams had passed the word on to the president. "That SEAL team leader on the ground, that Lieutenant Wazziz-name . . ."

"Lawlor, Sir, Lieutenant Lawlor," the admiral said.

"Yeah. Lawlor. That man's got balls. What a great military we have! The American people don't appreciate what a great military we have."

"No, sir, they don't," Gordon Jones, the secretary of defense, agreed.

"Right. Now this Lawlor guy, he'd make a great businessman. Weighs the risks, then takes action. Good man! Make a great businessman."

* * * * *

He had delayed it as long as he dared, but there were the still the nine other people on the ground to think about. Reluctantly, Clegg gave the order to scramble the helicopters.

Aboard the *Harry S. Truman*, three Navy MH60R "Seahawk" helicopters took off from the flight deck and headed northwest.

Only one of the choppers was needed to transport the six liberated missionaries and the SEAL team from the beach and back to the *Truman*, but one was to be held in reserve, and the other was a gunship, outfitted with a M240G machine gun, which fired a lethal, belt-fed, 7.62 mm NATO round. The Airedale Navy flew the helicopter, but a Marine manned the gun.

The pilots were highly skilled in the operation of these aircraft, and were instructed to go in low over the water, and low overland to the extraction zone to stay under what was most likely a Russian-built Nebo SVU "counter stealth" search radar, probably operating either at the Konarak air base, or the Iranian UAV launch facility. The Navy chopper pilots had trained, using their radar altimeters, to expertly follow the terrain, staying just four or five feet off the water, or off the ground, even at night.

The three helicopters were expected to be at the extraction site by 2350.

38

A Trip to the City

Konarak

Janelli didn't have to hotwire the Mercedes. The last driver had conveniently left the key in the ignition.

"I'm goin' with you, L-T," Cole said.

"No you're not, Billy. You need to stay here and be in charge. Get the troops and ferry the missionaries to the evac point. Use the Toyota. It's not far, but it's a longer walk than, at least, Mary Rogers can make."

"And what are we supposed to do if the choppers have to leave and you're not back? Just *leave* you here? You and Tindal? Just *desert* you?"

"You'll do exactly what you know you have to do, Chief, and you know it. You'll cut your losses and get everyone out that you can. And I'm telling you now—no, I'm *ordering* you— to evac with them." He knew Cole well enough to interpret that look. "I'm dead serious Billy, you stick with them. You know I'm right about this. And you know I would do exactly the same thing in your place." But Cole's look now said that he knew Jake would never "do exactly the same thing" in his place.

"Okay, Cole replied, "let's just say I give you that. But why not take one of us with you? Someone with the skills to watch your back. Take Fowles or Wilson, if you won't let me go."

"No need and no point. Two unfriendlies there at most. Bad enough I have to take Tindal with me . . . Time's a' wastin,' Gotta move. And Billy . . ."

"Yeah?"

"Drag those three bodies inside the prison, and out of sight. Daylight comes, we don't need to raise any alarms before we have to."

"Roger that, L-T. That we can do. Get right on it."

Jake got into the Mercedes. John Tindal was already in the passenger's seat. With the reactivated satellite radio to his ear, Jake said, "Exodus Base, this is Exodus Alfa, over."

"This is Base. Go ahead Alfa. Over." Clegg sounded as if he had gotten over his mad. Jake still knew that Clegg wouldn't cut him any slack if he ever got back home, but he also knew that Clegg would do his best to get Clare and John Tindal back safely with the others. And right now, that meant guiding Jake to the VIP's hotel.

"Alfa is headed out to the main road now, Base. Please proceed to vector me to objective site. Over."

"Roger that, Alfa . . ."

C2 then transmitted driving instructions, directing Jake to the colonel's hotel.

Ten minutes later, the Mercedes was in town and parked in front of the hotel. It was just 2328, and the street outside the hotel was already deserted. Apparently not much happened in Konarak after 10:00 PM in the off-season.

"This is definitely the place," Tindal said. "I recognize that sign."

"You can read that script?" Jake asked, surprised.

"No, I can speak the language but I can't read it. What I can read, and recognize, is the word 'hotel' in English at the bottom of the sign."

"Right," Jake said, feeling foolish. "You sit tight. I'm going in."

"No, you need me. I know which room she's in."

"So you said. Third floor, turn right, second last door on the left."

"Okay . . . but you can't speak the language. There's probably a night clerk in there. I can ask him to give you the room key."

"All right. You have a point. You can come in as far as the lobby. But only as far as the lobby. You stay there and wait, okay? Got it?"

"Got it."

Inside the hotel there was indeed a night clerk behind the counter. Fast asleep. Jake jarred him awake, and Tindal, in Farsi, began demanding the key to Clare's room. Jake could only get the gist of the conversation, but the clerk apparently answered that he needed more information, such as an actual room number. Jake saw Tindal point to him and his weapon, apparently threatening the clerk with dire consequences if he didn't cooperate. The clerk looked up at Jake, then at Tindal, and responded more respectfully to his questions thereafter.

Apparently, Tindal described the room's location to the clerk, since the conversation included Tindal pointing to the stairwell, and upward. Sheepishly, the clerk stood up and took down a key from the board behind the desk and handed it to Tindal, who, in turn, gave it to Jake.

"Ask him how many other guests there are in the hotel," Jake said.

Tindal asked, and the clerk made a lengthy reply.

"What'd he say?" Jake asked.

"He says there are a hundred and eight guest rooms, but it's off-season, and only forty-one are occupied. Most of the occupied rooms are here on the first floor. Only ten are occupied on the second, and three on the third. Apparently, two of the occupied rooms on the third floor are Clare's room and the colonel's suite. The suite on the opposite end of the third floor is also occupied, by a honeymooning couple."

Jake then sat the clerk back down and zip-tied him to the chair. He would have liked to have had a strip of Bonsignore's duct tape available about then, to gag the man, but time was of the essence, so instead he had to be content with having Tindal warn the man to be quiet.

"You are to stay here," Jake reminded Tindal. "And you watch him, knock him out if you have to, but keep him quiet." Tindal nodded in assent, as did, for some reason, the night clerk, and Jake walked over to the stairwell.

Ascending to the third-floor landing, and crouching low with his M4a1 at the ready, Jake peered around the corner to his right. The guard was at the end of the hallway, sitting on a straight-backed chair, in front of the next-to-the-last door on the left. The man was wide awake, and was mumbling under his breath as he read from the book he was holding. His head was turned a bit to his left and away from Jake, the book held so as to take advantage of the meager light from a sconce mounted on the wall at the very end of the hall. Jake saw no evidence of a weapon, but knew that there had to be one somewhere within reach.

Rising from a crouch, Jake tip-toed toward the seated guard. He was almost on top of him when the man sensed his presence, looked up, and saw Jake. He quickly reached for the rifle leaning against the wall to the left of his chair, but Jake, using the butt of his rifle, hit the man on his right temple, hard.

The guard fell over, unconscious, taking his chair and the almost-but-not-quite-attained rifle with him, making far more noise than Jake would have liked.

Working quickly, Jake moved the rifle well out of the man's reach. Then he zip-tied the man's wrists behind him and to the chair. Similarly, the man's ankles were secured to the chair legs. Again, Jake wished he had some of Bonsignore's duct tape. But if the guard woke up and started yelling, he could raise havoc. So, instead, using his Ka-bar, he cut some strips of cloth from the guard's shirt and improvised a gag. Then he put the key the night clerk had surrendered into the lock, and turned it. He had worried that it might not be the right key, and that he might have to break down the door, and make even more of a racket. But the latch clicked free, and Jake slowly pushed the door open.

* * * * *

On the floor below, Hamid, the light sleeper, awoke to the sound of the commotion on the floor overhead. He dressed quickly, and retrieved his G19 Glock 9mm Luger (completely illegal in Iran), and loaded a round into the chamber. He opened the door to his suite, saw that the hallway was clear, and made his way slowly down the hall to the stairwell.

39

At the Extraction Zone

Konarak

It took two trips with the Toyota to transport the four missionaries and Cole's four men to the extraction site. Cole first supervised getting Mary Rogers onto the truck bed, where she could lie flat, with her husband and Slewfoot Wilson attending her. He and Bonsignore drove out to the designated spot two klicks west of the prison. Leaving Mary Rogers wrapped in a blanket and lying on the ground on a second blanket, Cole left his men there on guard, then drove back and got the others. Not long afterward, the nine of them were there waiting for the choppers from the *Truman* to arrive.

Soon enough, Cole could hear the *wumpp! wumpp!* of the choppers approaching from the southeast. It was 2333. Cole's satellite radio was tuned to the HF frequency the helos were using, and he soon heard, "Exodus Alfa, this is Exodus One. Over."

"This is Exodus Bravo, Exodus Alfa is busy. Over."

"This is One. Roger that, Exodus Bravo. Hell of a fine mess you've made, Bravo! Your Base informs we have only a partial shipment. Over"

"Roger that, One, but we have eight souls ready for immediate evac. One soul needs immediate medical attention as soon as she can get it. Over."

"Roger that. But Base informed first shipment was to be niner, I say again, *niner* souls, over." (*All U.S. military radio protocol follows NATO rules, and since the number "nine" sounds the same as the German "nein," for "no," the number nine is always spoken as "niner" to avoid any confusion.*)

"Negative, One. This Exodus Bravo goes only when Exodus Alfa and two remaining packages are ready for transport. Over."

"Gotcha, Bravo. Base will be unhappy, but One will take what he can get and skedaddle. Approaching landing site. Out."

A half-minute later, a Navy Seahawk settled down for a landing; even winding down, the rotor downdraft sending sand and pebbles flying everywhere. The two other choppers stood off, remaining airborne.

Cole saw to it, with the help of the crew aboard the helicopter, that Mary Rogers was first aboard, followed by Wilson and her husband, and then the Crowleys. Fowles, Bonsignore, and Janelli put up an argument against joining them until Jake and the Tindals returned, but Cole made it an order, and they had no choice but to obey it. With all eight boarded, then, Cole slapped the side of the helicopter hard, and shouted into the radio, "You're good to go, One."

"Roger that. I have orders to return to base," came the barely audible reply, "but Exodus Two and Three will stay behind as long as possible."

Cole backed away from the rotor wash as the engines wound up. "Understood, One," Cole replied, using the radiophone. "Have a safe trip. Over."

"Roger that and good luck, Bravo. One, out." And the helicopter lifted off, turned in place to the southeast, and headed off toward the gulf.

When the first chopper was well clear, Cole heard a female voice over the radio. "Bravo, this is Two, over."

The gunship (Exodus Three) was still airborne, hovering overhead. It was just 2342.

"Bravo, over."

"Coming in, Bravo, Two out."

Another Seahawk landed, this time completely shutting down its engines. Cole walked up to the open doorway as the rotors were still spinning down.

"Welcome to Konarak, Ma'am, gentlemen," Cole shouted up to the pilot and her crew.

"Cut the crap, Chief," the pilot laughingly retorted. "All we want to do is get back to our nice, friendly, carrier, and the sooner the better."

"I hear that, Ma'am," Cole answered. "Just waiting on my lieutenant and two missionaries."

"They better hurry, Chief. That gunship goes bingo [has just enough fuel left to make it safely back to the carrier] in less than a half-hour, and my orders are to leave with him, with or without any packages."

"Understood, Ma'am. Understood."

* * * * *

In the situation room, the president was very unhappy. He was staring at the infrared presentation piped in from the surveillance drone to the plasma screen, and could just about figure out what was happening on the ground in Konarak.

None of the red "hot spots" appeared to have moved for some minutes, not since the one left the prison site and headed south.

"Will somebody please tell me what the hell is happening?" he complained.

"Well, Mr. President—" Williams began, but the secretary of defense, Gordon Jones, jumped in and interrupted him.

"The Navy chopper is waiting at the extraction site with the SEAL team Chief, Mr. President, and the gunship is in the air overhead, protecting them. Meanwhile, Lt. Lawlor and her husband are still in the town attempting to retrieve Mrs. Tindal."

"Good," the president replied, "She's Longstreet's daughter. Not saying the others weren't important, mind you, but if it weren't for Longstreet, we would probably still be twiddling our thumbs, still trying to come up with a plan to get our people back. Be a damn shame if we couldn't get her out of there after all! A really terrible shame!"

Jones pointed to a fading red glow in the town. "This is the automobile they took into town. When it starts moving again, it means they're on their way back to the extraction zone. So far it hasn't moved."

"Why doesn't one of the damn helicopters just go in and get 'em?" the president asked.

"Because, Sir, the noise would awaken the whole town, and the helos would never get out of Iran in one piece."

"Why is that?"

"'Cause the entire Iranian Air Force would be on top of them before they could clear Iranian airspace.

"But the good news, Sir," Jones continued, "is that eight of our people, including four of the missionaries, are on the helicopter that just cleared Iranian airspace and are over international waters. They'll be safely aboard the *Truman* in just a matter of minutes."

"Damn," the president exclaimed to no one in particular, "But what we need to do is what we started out to do: get *all* our people safely the hell out of there. Every last one of them."

"Roger that, Mr. President," Jones agreed.

"Damn," the president said again.

40

Confrontation

Konarak

Salehrad awoke to some commotion in the hallway outside the door to his suite. He rose from the bed, and grabbed his 9 mm pistol, an unlicensed Iranian copy of the Swiss SIG Sauer P226, from off the nightstand. He customarily slept in his underwear, on top of the covers, and now felt undressed and vulnerable. The noises that awoke him could be nothing at all, but they could also signify the presence of an intruder.

He sat on side of the bed and gathering his wits, his ears pricked, alert to any additional sounds coming from the hallway. All was silent for a while, and Salehrad had almost decided that the noise was just part of a dream. He had nearly set his pistol back on the nightstand and laid back down, when he heard the unmistakable click of a latch being released and a door being opened close by.

Now he was unwilling to even take the time to find the terrycloth bathrobe the hotel provided its guests. He crept barefoot, in his underwear, to the door to his suite, and, pistol at the ready, slowly opened the door and peered out into the hallway.

Even in the dim light, he could see that the man who had guarded Clare Tindal's room was now lying on his side and affixed to a chair. His man appeared unconscious, and might even possibly be dead. But he was more concerned about the person or persons who had disabled the guard, than he was about the man himself.

Salehrad stuck his head out into the hallway just enough to see that Clare Tindal's door was open, and he could hear low-pitched voices coming from the room. He knew exactly what he must do next. He quietly shut the door to his room, and turning on the suite's overhead light, quickly went to the door that connected his sitting room to Clare Tindal's room.

* * * * *

"How sure are you that your lieutenant is coming?" the pilot of Exodus Two asked.

"He's a SEAL, Ma'am, the best of the best. And he's my friend. If anyone can get those people back here safe, it's him," Cole replied.

"If we run out of time, Chief, and we have to leave here, you're not planning on coming with us, are you?" She said it more as a statement than as a question.

"Don't think so, Ma'am. No, probably not."

No, she thought, definitely *not.* Then she said aloud, "Well, then you'd just better pray he makes it. He's got maybe another ten minutes."

"Oh, he'll make it all right, Ma'am. I know he'll make it. I just don't know if he'll make it in ten minutes or not."

* * * * *

"Nothing's happening. What the hell is going on over there? None of the red spots on the screen are moving! Nothing's happening!"

"You know as much as we do, Mr. President. We have no way of knowing what's going on in that hotel. And if Lawlor and the Tindals are in trouble, there's nothing we can do to help them," Gordon Jones replied.

"What about the other SEAL on the ground? Wazziz name?"

"Chief Cole, sir, William Cole. We could send him after Lawlor, Mr. President, but there's no guarantee if Lawlor and the Tindals have been taken out, that he could do anything about it beyond confirming what had happened, and possibly even being taken out himself."

"What a shitty situation! We're gonna come out of this thing looking like a bunch of bumbling idiots. Jimmy Carter and that embassy hostage rescue thing all over again! They'll be a real shit storm over this if Lawlor and Cole can't come through, Gordy, a real shit storm!"

"But Mr. President," Jones said, "four of the six American missionaries are safely aboard the carrier. That much of the operation, at least, is a complete success."

"Not good enough, Gordy, not good enough at all. It's still a shitty situation," the president observed, "and we need to bring all of them home. All of them!"

* * * * *

Just before Hamid reached the stairwell, he saw an unknown man wearing a filthy orange jumpsuit pass in front of him and start to ascend the stairway to the third floor of the hotel. Hamid followed silently after him, Glock still at the ready.

41

Resolution

Konarak

Clare Tindal's room was dark, and the light coming in from the hallway was totally useless. Jake pulled his night vision gear down and peered over at the bed. It was empty. M4a1 at the ready, he crept further into the room.

"Who are you?" a voice said that came from Jake's left, just beyond the foot of the bed. Turning quickly toward the voice, he saw the ghostly green form of a woman, apparently in nightclothes, sitting in the dark.

"I'm Navy Lieutenant Lawlor, Ma'am. Jake Lawlor. Your husband is waiting for us downstairs, and we've come to take you home."

"Praise God!" she said. "You say John is downstairs and waiting for us?"

"Yes, Ma'am, he is." He waited a few seconds to let the news sink in. "Come along now, Ma'am, we have to move quickly, if we're gonna get you and Mr. Tindal home."

"Home," she repeated, just as the adjoining door that connected her room to the colonel's suite opened wide, and light flooded into the room. Framed in the doorway was the colonel himself, and Clare could just make out the pistol in his hand.

"Colonel!" she warned.

The sudden influx of light blinded Jake's night vision gear, and he had to flip it up in order to see. At the same time he had to turn and face this new threat while bringing his rifle to bear. And he almost made it.

Salehrad fired three shots in succession. Jake was three-quarters of the way into his turn, and the first 9 mm bullet plowed a furrow in his upper right arm. The second struck him point-blank as he completed his turn, full in the chest, , knocking him backward off his feet. The third round struck the stock of his M4a1, as he began his fall, blasting it out of his grasp, and sending it over his head and skittering across the floor, where it stopped abruptly at Clare Tindal's feet.

Clare saw that the colonel, barefoot and in his underwear, kept his pistol pointed at Jake as he advanced into the room.

Reaching Jake, Salehrad gazed down at his prey, satisfied and pleased with what he saw. The man obviously was incapacitated, if not dead, and bleeding where his bullet had almost ripped the American flag patch off his fatigues.

John Tindal, rushing toward the commotion, then appeared and stuck his head into the doorway. "Clare?" he shouted.

Salehrad looked up from his victory and turned to face this new threat, pistol at the ready. But when he saw that the intruder was wearing an orange jump suit, he held his fire. He quickly assessed just who it was — John Tindal — and he was not going to jeopardize his mission by shooting one of the missionaries he was supposed to make confess to espionage.

Clare Tindal looked down at the rifle at her feet. It looked very different from the hunting rifle with which she had become so proficient. Yet it still had a barrel, a stock, and a trigger. The colonel had just probably killed the American soldier who had come to help them, take them home. And now, John, her husband, was in trouble; and the man she now hated so much was pointing his pistol at him.

Clare quickly leaned over, and, without really thinking about it, picked up the rifle, pointed it at the colonel, and squeezed the trigger. The M4a1 fires only in automatic. In just squeezing and holding the trigger down for what she thought was a split second, a dozen 5.56 mm bullets flew at the colonel. *Brrrrrrrrrap!* The very first one struck him in the chest, the second pierced his skull just to the right, and above, his left eye, and the remaining ten sprayed off into the room behind him, lodging in the far wall. But the two bullets that had struck the man were sufficient. Salehrad was dead before his body hit the floor.

Clare, now horrified at what had just happened — what *she* had just done — gingerly set the rifle back down on the floor. A few seconds later, John Tindal walked slowly into the room, he too, now dazed and overwhelmed by what he had just witnessed: his wife had just shot a man to death.

"Clare?" he asked.

"It's okay, John," she answered. "I'm okay. But we need to see to the soldier. I think maybe he's dead."

Hamid had heard the shots, of course, and now cautiously approached the doorway, peering inside. But he was able to assess the scene quickly. Even in the poor lighting, he could see that none of the three living occupants were armed, although there was a rifle on the floor in front of the woman.

Hamid found the light switch and turned it on. The woman in a nightgown was standing in front of a sofa, and the man in the dirty orange jump suit had walked over to her and was holding her. Both were sobbing. To his right, the colonel's body was stretched out on the floor, his eyes open, staring at the ceiling, a bloody hole blown in his forehead.

Has to be dead, Hamid thought. A man in fatigues, American from the torn patch on his sleeve, was also sprawled on the floor in front of him, but was now groaning, bleeding from his right arm. He needed immediate help. Hamid put his pistol in his waistband, and said, in English, to the Tindals, "Come, we must help the American."

"He's not dead?" Clare asked, now too disoriented to even question this new, unknown, person's presence.

"He's not dead, possibly just dazed." Hamid replied, and repeated, "But we must help him! We need to get something to stop the bleeding. A tourniquet." Hamid looked around the room, saw a lamp on a side table, and unplugged the electric cord. He tried to pull the cord from the lamp, but it wouldn't budge.

John Tindal, meanwhile, had gone over to Jake, and had helped him sit up. Jake, still dazed, had somehow conjured up a picture of Julie in his mind. His mind, he thought, was in a good place, and he wanted to stay there — enjoy this time with Julie — but then he realized, suddenly, that he had to will himself awake. He couldn't remember exactly what it was, but there was something important he had to do.

Coming fully awake, and shaking the cobwebs from his brain, Jake saw, and quickly realized, that there was a newcomer in the room.

"This electric cord in just the thing for a tourniquet," the newcomer explained to no one in particular, "But I cannot get the cord free of the lamp!"

Judging this newcomer to be a friendly, Jake said, "Here," drawing and extending his Ka-bar to him. Hamid took the knife and sliced through the cord at the lamp base, then tied the cord around Jake's upper arm, just above the wound, fixing it with a square knot.

Hamid surveyed the room again, and spied a ballpoint pen lying next to a pad on the nightstand. Using the pen, he twisted the cord.

"Damn," Jake said, "not too tight. Help me up. We've got to get out of here, or we'll miss our ride."

"Grab the lieutenant's gun, Clare," John said, pointing to the M4a1. "We may need it." And he went over to where Hamid was tending to Jake's arm.

Hamid, satisfied with the tourniquet, handed Jake's Ka-bar back to him. "Give me some help," he said to Tindal, and both men began to help Jake to his feet.

"I think I can walk," Jake said, but the two men continued to give him support. Clare led them into the hallway, brandishing Jake's rifle, as the foursome made its way down the hall, and down to the stairwell.

At the second-floor landing, Hamid asked, "Is the night clerk alive and awake?"

"He is," John Tindal affirmed.

"Of course he is," Hamid said. "Then here I must leave you. It would not be good for the night clerk to see me. He will recognize me."

"Who are you?" John Tindal asked.

"Just a friend," Hamid answered. Then, to Jake, "Do you think you can make it from here?"

"Yeah," Jake said. "I think we can make it from here." And then to the Tindals, "But we'll have to hurry, or we'll be stuck here forever without a ride home."

"*Shalom,*" Hamid said, and turned and left them, heading back to his suite.

"*Shalom,*" Jake called back after him.

215

It took the three of them a good while to finally get to the Mercedes, and the night clerk, still bound to his chair, watched them leave the building, but remained silent. The colonel's woman, after all, was wielding that big gun. Only after the trio had left the building, and he was sure they were well out of earshot, did he finally shout out for help. But no one came.

John Tindal drove, Clare rode shotgun (literally), and Jake gave directions back to Qajar from the back seat.

42

Extraction Site

Konarak

"Exodus Two, this is Three. I'm bingo. You comin' or not? Over!"

"Three, Bravo won't budge, and unhappy about going without him. I promised him ten minutes. Over."

Yeah, Cole thought, *but that was over ten minutes ago.*

"Two, I can't give you *one* minute. Our orders are now for the two of us to leave together. And if we don't leave ASAP, I'll be swimming before we reach the barn, over."

"Roger that, Three. Out." Then to Cole, "Sorry, Chief, if they're not here and you're not coming with us, I've still got to go. Orders," she explained.

"Roger that, Ma'am. Have a safe flight." And Exodus Two restarted her helicopter's engines.

Once Exodus Two was airborne, she and the gunship turned southeast and headed out. It was 0020, and Jake and John Tindal had left for the hotel over an hour earlier.

* * * * *

"It's moving!" the president said, and pointed to the red dot on the screen that was the heat signature of the car in front of the hotel.

"Yes, it is, Sir," V.Adm. Williams said, and directly got on the secure line to C2 to tell them to get word out to the helicopters at the extraction site that the rest of their "packages" were on the way.

Williams had no sooner gotten off the line, when he saw from their heat signatures that both of the helicopters were already departing the extraction site and were en route to the *Truman*. "I'm afraid it's too late, Mr. President. The helicopters have already left to return to the carrier. They were under orders to leave whenever the gunship went bingo."

"Bingo? the president asked, "what the hell is bingo?"

The Admiral explained "bingo" to the president, as they watched the heat signature of the Mercedes speed toward the extraction site. But the last train had already left Liberty Junction.

* * * * *

Cole left the extraction site, and drove the Toyota back to the prison. He had no doubt that Jake would eventually return with the Tindals. But their ride was already gone. And Jake hadn't pulled this particular miracle off, after all.

Off to the east, there finally appeared a distant bloom of light, undoubtedly from approaching headlights. As the light became more distinct, and the headlights themselves were distinguishable, he thought: *Looks like now we'll have to come up with a plan B!*

The Mercedes pulled up two minutes later.

* * * * *

The first elements of the Konarak fishing fleet were just leaving Chabahar Bay and entering the Gulf of Oman when the throbbing sound of a helicopter passing overhead disturbed the silence of the night. The fishermen searched the sky in the direction of Exodus Three's rotor noise, looking for the airship's navigation lights, but there were none. Then another, similarly unlit, helicopter passed overhead. Despite the fact that the choppers were flying in the wrong direction for it, four of the more patriotic individual boat captains notified the Iranian Air Force of a possible enemy invasion. One such alarm might have been ignored, but not four. Within thirty-eight minutes, scrambled jets from the Konarak Airfield were in the air looking for intruders, but by that time Exodus Two and Three were already out over international waters.

It was only after the choppers were approaching the *Truman* to land, that the pilots received the word relayed from C2 that the vehicle from town was on its way, and to wait for it. *A day late and a dollar short,* thought the Exodus Two pilot. *Godspeed, Exodus Bravo,* she prayed. *I sure hope you make it home somehow, Chief.*

* * * * *

"How in hell could we have left four people in Iran?" the president, furious, asked the dignitaries in the situation room. "How could we have let that happen? All the damn helicopters had to do was wait! Let's get another 'copter to them, now!"

"Can't do that, Mr. President," Gordon Jones explained. "When the choppers left the area, the Iranians got word of it— God only knows how. An Air Force drone picked up a flight of six military jets combing the skies, looking for trouble. Our choppers were barely gone from Iranian air space when they arrived, thank God, but it would be suicide to send in another chopper now."

The president let out a string of expletives.

43

Stuck

Konarak

"Exodus Base, this is Exodus Alfa, over."

"This is Base, go ahead, Alfa."

"Looks like we missed our ride, Base, but 'packages' are secure, over."

Secure for the time being, anyway, Jake thought.

"Roger that, Alfa, Base is working on an alternative extraction plan now, over."

"Roger that, but be advised that we have apparently alerted the cavalry. Jets buzzing overhead. We'll try to make ourselves less conspicuous while Base works on a plan. Over."

"Roger, Alfa. Will notify you when we have alternate plan, over."

"Negative, Base, your initiation of transmissions probably not a good idea if enemy is anywhere within earshot. Propose we check in on even hours, local time, if clear to transmit. Do you concur? Over."

"Understand, Alfa, and concur. Will look for your transmission on even hours, your time. Stay safe. Over."

"Roger that, Base, Alfa, out."

Then Jake turned the radio off to save the battery, and told Cole to do that same with his.

"First we have to do something about your arm, L-T, and then we do something about these outfits. In these fatigues, we stick out like sore thumbs," Cole said. "We need to get some medical supplies, and either find a place to hide, or get a change of clothes, or even better, do both."

"Well, Qajar is probably secure for the time being. Let's see what they have inside."

The Tindals, reluctant to ever again cross Qajar's threshold, asked if they could stay outside while Cole and Jake went into the prison. Jake said they could, but only if they stayed out of sight, and inside the Mercedes. They agreed, and the SEALs went into Qajar, and rummaged around until Cole said "There!" pointing to cabinet marked with a red crescent, mounted on the wall next to the kitchen sink. Inside was medical supplies.

Jake had been studiously easing off on the tourniquet every fifteen minutes or so since Hamid had originally tightened it, and each time the wound had bled less and less. When Cole eased off the tourniquet to clean and bandage the wound, the bleeding had stopped almost completely.

"Don't think you'll need this anymore, L-T," Cole said, referring to the tourniquet, but, still, he pocketed the device, just in case the bleeding recurred. Then he cleaned and bandaged the wound, closing it as best he could with some butterfly bandages. "I think you're good to go, for now," Cole said, finally, admiring his work. "But you should probably have some stitches. That, I'm afraid, is a bit out of my league."

"Time enough for stitches later," Jake said, as Cole finished the job by wrapping his arm with gauze.

All the while, the two SEALs could hear the bound men on the second floor struggling to free themselves.

Once again outside Qajar, the two SEALs got into the Mercedes with the Tindals and laid out a plan of action.

44

What Are Friends For?

Washington, D.C., Tel Aviv, Konarak

"Hello, Helen, to what do I owe this unexpected pleasure?" said Shlomo Rosenszweig, speaking over the secure line to Washington, D.C.

"I apologize for calling you so late, Moe. I know it's after midnight there, but we've run into a bit of a problem in Iran, and I thought you might be able to help," Helen Siebert said.

"Not at all, Helen. You know *you* can call me anytime. What is the situation in Iran?" (Rosenszweig already knew from his own sources that an American extraction team had landed in Iran, but knew nothing yet of their progress.)

"Well, Moe, as usual, both good and bad news. The good news is that we've successfully extracted four of the six American missionaries the Iranians were holding. The bad news is that we still have four people in country there—two of the missionaries and two Navy SEALs. They're free for the time being, but we've stirred up a real hornet's nest now, and we need to get them out before they get caught, and we've got an even bigger international incident on our hands."

"Understood." Rosenszweig said, and paused in thought. "All right, Helen, you are aware we have a man on the ground there. He's one of our very best, but I am not at all sure how he can help. At least not for the moment. Let me contact him and see what he can do." Another pause. "And Helen?"

"Yes?"

"Is there any way he can contact your people — speak to them directly?"

"They have satellite radiotelephones, and are checking in every two hours. And I'm sure you have your own secure voice communications with your man in the field. It should be possible to link them up, but that's well outside my field of expertise."

"And mine," Rosenszweig said. "But I can give you a name and a number on my end, and you can work with your people to make that happen."

* * * * *

Jake thought it more prudent to leave the Mercedes parked where they originally found it at the prison, and to drive the far less recognizable Toyota into town instead. Cole and John Tindal rode in the truck bed, while Jake drove, and Clare, again, rode shotgun.

Jake parked the truck in front of a clothing store in the old town. It was 0133 local time and the street was deserted. The sign on the corner had read Khadija St. in English under the Persian script.

Cole got out and picked the lock on the door. He opened it slowly, ready to bolt if an alarm sounded. There was none. Apparently robbing clothing stores was not a regular occurrence in Konarak. The four went inside, and within a half hour were all wearing civilian street clothes. Jake and Cole managed to stuff their uniforms and gear into their backpacks. Unfortunately, their rifles were too big to fit inside. They could hardly walk about town in the daylight carrying rifles, but they wouldn't have to face that problem until morning. Meanwhile, if they were caught wearing civilian clothes and were out of uniform, day or night, they would be hanged as spies. But they figured that if they were ever captured, in or out of uniform, to the Iranians, that would be a mere detail.

At 0200, Jake turned his radiotelephone on and checked in with C2.

"Exodus Base, this is Exodus Alfa. Over."

"This is Base, go ahead Alfa. Over."

"We are in the city and have secured civilian clothes for all parties. Any word on extraction? Over."

"Wait one, Alfa. Am patching you into a local."

Jake waited. Then came, "Hello . . . Lieutenant?"

"Yes?"

"*Shalom.*" And Jake knew immediately who the "local" was.

"*Shalom,*" Jake responded.

"Where are you, Lieutenant?"

"In a clothing store on, wait one, I have to check the street sign." Jake strode to the front of the store and searched for the street sign. "We're on Khadija Street."

"Ah, yes. Named after the Prophet's first wife. I know just where that is. Stand fast. I will come to you."

"We'll be waiting." Then, "You get all that, Base?"

"Roger that. Expect you're in good hands. Check back in two hours. Base, out."

Jake turned the phone off again after checking its remaining battery capacity. The battery supposedly had over half of its charge remaining.

At 0216, a Porsche Boxter pulled up in front of the store and parked behind the Toyota. Jake immediately recognized the casually dressed, and dapper-looking Middle Easterner, who stepped out of the car.

45

Down Time

Konarak

"Hello, again." Jake greeted the man who drove the Porsche with a smile.

"Hello, Lieutenant," Hamid replied. "And so we meet once more. How is your arm?"

"Hurts like hell, but I'll live. The tourniquet got the bleeding under control, thanks to you. Chief Cole, here," Jake pointed him out, "cleaned me up and bandaged me."

"Well, the wound looked pretty deep, but the bullet passed through," Hamid said, "and you weren't losing any arterial blood. You should be okay for now. But some stitches and some antibiotics would probably be good."

"They probably would at that," Jake agreed. "But I don't think I'll be checking into any of the local clinics."

Hamid smiled. "No," he said, "that would probably not be a good idea. We had best get you back to your own people for that."

"I'm Jake," Jake said and extended his hand. Hamid took it, shook it, and covered both their right hands with his left. He smiled warmly, as if Jake were an old and admired friend.

"And I am Hamid. And these others? We met back at the hotel, but I do not know their names."

"John and Clare Tindal. They're two of the Americans we came here to rescue."

John and Clare nodded to Hamid.

"And the other four prisoners?" Hamid asked.

"They're fine. Probably well on their way home by now. We four would have left with them, except for tangling up with that SAVAK colonel back at the hotel."

"Well, then," Hamid explained, "your people have asked my people to help get you home. I am fairly certain I can see you transported safely out into the gulf. I have to assume that once in international waters, your own people can pick you up?"

"And I'm fairly certain that can be arranged," Jake replied. "So, okay, how will you get us out into the Gulf?"

"By boat. I can get you all to the boat tonight, but the man who owns and drives the boat will not be joining us until the morning. You will have to spend the night aboard, I am afraid."

Now John Tindal laughed. "I can assure you, Hamid, that no matter how uncomfortable your boat, that for the past several weeks we have slept in far worse places."

"As I can imagine," Hamid smiled back. "Now, to get to the boat. I'm afraid all five of us will not get into my car at the same time—"

"No need," Jake interrupted. "We can use the truck you parked behind."

"Excellent. But then I'd best park the Porsche back at the hotel. Follow me there."

Not too long afterward, riding crammed in the middle of the truck cab, with Jake driving, and sitting beside Clare Tindal, Hamid directed Jake down the plank road that was the dock. Once again, Cole and John Tindal rode in the truck bed.

Jake parked in front of the *Roya*. He peered up and down the dock, then got out of the truck, and peered up and down the dock again, but everything was dead quiet save the wind-driven ripples gently slapping against the dock pilings.

After settling the four Americans aboard *Roya*, and out of sight belowdecks, Hamid drove the Toyota back into town and parked it in a quiet street not too far from his hotel. He walked to the hotel, got the bicycle, and rode it back to the *Roya*. He was careful to announce himself before coming aboard, lest he drew fire from Billy Cole, who stood guard at the cabin door.

"And so we wait," he said to Cole, noting that despite their uncomfortable positions, the other three Americans were fast asleep.

"You didn't happen to find any food on the way here, did you?" Cole asked, half as a joke.

"No, sorry," Hamid answered. "But Amir, the boat owner, will most likely bring some with him when he arrives in the morning."

"Then Amir will be *very* welcome," Cole said. It was 0352, and Cole waited out the eight minutes for an 0400 report to C2.

"Exodus Base, this is Exodus Bravo. Over."

"This is Base. Expected Exodus Alfa to make report, Bravo. Is Alfa okay? Where is Alpha? Over."

"Alfa is resting, Base. Alfa was wounded while he was retrieving the lost package. He's okay for now, but needs stitches and antibiotics ASAP. Over."

"Roger Bravo. Obviously Alfa neglected to inform Base of that situation. Over."

"Roger Base." Cole thought it best to make no further reference to Jake's having been wounded. "Any word on extraction plan? Over."

"Affirmative. Base understands the local agent plans to transport you to the Gulf. Navy will pick you up there, once you're in international waters. Over."

"Roger that. The sooner we're out of here the better. Bravo, out."

46

Too Little, Too Late

Konarak

One of the two trucks bearing the platoon of twenty-eight Iranian Army Regulars had broken down on the way to Konarak, and both trucks had just pulled up in front of Qajar prison at 0412. It was still dark, with not a single light showing from the prison building, and military jets could be heard flying overhead. The driver of the lead truck pulled up behind the Mercedes that was parked in front of the place. The first lieutenant in charge of the platoon, who sat next to the driver in the cab, told him to sound the horn. There was no response.

"Someone should be awake and on guard," the first lieutenant said, sensing that something was very wrong.

By 0500 the Iranian first lieutenant had a fairly good picture of what had happened at Qajar prison.

Four of the SAVAK troops were known dead, three of whom were the men who had stood perimeter guard. Whoever had killed them had dragged their bodies from where they died at their posts, and laid them out neatly inside the prison. The fourth corpse was found in the basement. Recalling what he had seen there caused the first lieutenant to shudder involuntarily. The cage that had held the six prisoners was empty. From the three men found bound to their beds in the barracks room, he learned that the men had been attacked as they slept by Russians. And that the SAVAK colonel in charge of the operation, one of his men, and one of the prisoners, a woman, were in town at the hotel where the colonel was staying. (If the first lieutenant had any immediate questions as to why the colonel was staying at a hotel in town rather than at the prison, and why he had taken a woman there with him, he kept them to himself.)

One of the SAVAK troops that was found in the upstairs room knew the route to the hotel, and the first lieutenant planned on using him as a guide, and on going to the hotel himself to determine the situation there. But first he reported in to his superiors in Teheran and apprised them of the situation on the ground in Konarak. He was informed that some local fisherman en route to their fishing grounds had reported hearing helicopters overhead and heading out to sea about 0100. He was ordered to take enough men with him to handle whatever situation he found in town.

He loaded *all of* his regulars back into the transport trucks, and placed the SAVAK man in the cab of the lead truck to direct the driver to the hotel. It was 0554 when both vehicles reached the hotel.

The first lieutenant took four of his men inside the hotel with him and found the hotel night clerk asleep and bound to his chair behind the counter. Awakened and released, the clerk told whomever would listen about how badly he had been treated, and how an American soldier and a man in an orange jump suit had assaulted him. He told of the shots he had heard fired, and how the man in the orange jump suit, along with the woman for whom the colonel had rented the room adjoining

233

his suite, had helped the American soldier (who apparently had been hurt) back out to the street.

"What time did they leave the hotel?" the first lieutenant asked the night clerk.

"I'm not sure," he answered, "but I think it was around midnight. Perhaps later."

Remembering that the fishermen had reported hearing the helicopters overhead at 0100, the first lieutenant concluded, *Then they are long gone – but, then again – perhaps not.* He decided that once the situation here at the hotel was resolved, he would use his men to search the entire town and its surroundings for the Americans, just in case.

With the freed night clerk escorting the first lieutenant and his four men, they went cautiously up the stairs toward the third-floor rooms where the colonel and Clare Tindal had been staying. Outside, in the hallway, they found the SAVAK trooper who had stood guard dazed and disoriented, bound to his overturned chair, and his rifle some distance down the hall.

As his men released the guard, the first lieutenant entered the open doorway to Clare Tindal's room with his pistol drawn (ironically, the same model 9mm, Swiss SIG Sauer, P226 Iranian knock-off Salehrad had used).

From the doorway, he had seen the man sprawled on the floor, and the pool of blood drying under the body. The dead man was in his underwear, and the room was otherwise empty. The clerk identified the corpse as Colonel Salehrad.

Entering the colonel's suite by the adjoining doorway, the first lieutenant found the suite unoccupied, and the uniform of a SAVAK colonel hanging in the closet. He dispatched two of his men to knock on all the doors in the hotel to find out whatever any of the guests heard or saw during the night. He then called his superiors in Teheran and reported all that he had seen and heard. He was then told to let the local police handle the situation from there, and to return to Qajar and await further orders.

The first lieutenant tactfully suggested to his superiors that the three Americans who had murdered the SAVAK colonel might *not* have been evacuated after all, and that they could still possibly be in the area. Relenting, his superiors authorized a search of the city and its surrounding area.

The two men who had surveyed the hotel guests returned and reported that, first, there were very few guests in the hotel, and, second, those who answered their door reported that they had seen and heard nothing whatever during the night.

Impossible, the lieutenant thought, *but then, after all, this* is *Iran.* He then split his platoon up into two groups. He placed half of his men in one of the trucks, along with the SAVAK man, and under the command of the platoon's first sergeant. These he sent back to Qajar to scour the area around the prison. He left the lead truck parked in the street outside the hotel, split his remaining troops up in groups of two, and directed a street-by-street search of the entire city. It was 0545.

On the drive back to the prison, the first sergeant's transport truck passed two modestly-dressed women on bicycles headed in the same direction.

47

Dockside

Konarak

At 0547, Cole shook Jake awake. He had been dreaming about black cats and pretty Italian-American girls.

"What's going on?" Jake asked groggily.

"Nothing. Thought you might want to call in to C2."

"Okay. Is it 0400 already?"

Cole chuckled. "No, L-T, it's going on 0600."

"We were supposed to report at 0400."

"It's okay. I reported in. Told C2 that we were waiting for a boat ride out into the Gulf. C2 said they would arrange for a pickup whenever we reached international waters." He purposely neglected to tell Jake that he had informed C2 that Jake was wounded.

"Okay, good. That brought them up to speed anyway. Is Hamid back? Any activity outside?"

"Hamid's over there, asleep. I'm to awaken him when I hear a moped comin' down the dock. That would be Amir, the guy who owns this tub. Supposed to be here around 0700. And, no, outside it's been as quiet as a mouse since the Iranian Air Force stopped buzzing the town with their jets."

"When did *that* stop?"

"About 0300 or so. Think they've given up on us?"

"No idea. There's supposed to be some Navy patrol boats tied up out here. Any activity from them?"

"Not that I've seen or heard. Maybe they *have* given up on us. That would be logical enough. There's no way they could have known that we missed our ride."

"Let's hope you're right. I'll report in." Jake turned on his radiotelephone. "Exodus Base, this is Exodus Alfa, over."

"This is Base, go ahead, Alfa."

"We are awaiting arrival of our boat driver. Supposed to be here 0700 local time. Over."

"Roger that, Alfa. How is your wound holding up? Over."

Billy Cole, thought Jake, *you SOB, you ratted me out!* "Alfa will probably live, Base. It's not too bad. Over."

"Very Well. Navy has Sierra Bravo Tango ready to dispatch whenever you are ready. Keep us informed. Base Out."

Sierra Bravo Tango, Jake thought. *SBT – a special boat team. Manned by a Special Weapons Combat-craft Crew. The SWCC was only Navy organization recruited by, manned by, and administered entirely by Navy enlisted men. Come get us, guys!*

Not too long after that, the high-pitched whine of a moped engine could be heard coming down the dock.

48

Leadership House

Teheran

It was just after 7:00 AM. The Supreme Leader was seething, and Dariush knew enough to keep his distance. They were in the conference room, and the Supreme Leader had summoned the entire Guardianship Council to Leadership House for an emergency meeting.

Earlier, at six that morning, after the situation on the ground in Konarak had become clear, the Supreme Leader had been awakened. The major general in command of the Islamic Republic of Iran Army (IRIA) personally reported to him concerning the events that had gone down during the night.

The major general reported that the regular army platoon had arrived on the scene at Qajar prison about 4:00 AM after traveling all day. By five-thirty, the officer-in-charge of the platoon reported what he had discovered: an apparent CIA operation had staged a raid at the prison, murdered four of the guards, and freed the only five Americans who were still being held at the prison.

One of the American women was missing, and apparently the SAVAK colonel in charge of the operation had absconded with the woman to a nearby hotel for his own purposes. The

CIA operatives then raided the hotel, killed the colonel, and made off with the woman.

It was most probable that all six of the American prisoners were then whisked off by helicopter — probably to an American ship at sea. But, on the *slim* chance that the woman being used by the SAVAK colonel, and the CIA operatives who had gone after her had not, in fact, been evacuated, the army was conducting a house-to-house search for them in Konarak, and in the area around Qajar prison. But the IRIA commander held out little hope to the Supreme Leader of any prospect for the success of that endeavor.

Those fools at SAVAK were so certain the Americans had no idea whatever as to where we were holding their people! the Supreme Leader thought. *I am surrounded with gross incompetence! That fool running SAVAK will be the first to pay. He will pay not only for being duped by the Americans, but also for the deaths of four faithful Iranian martyrs, and for the illicit actions of the man he placed in charge. Allah has, at least, seen to it that this Colonel Salehrad has paid for his crimes!* The Supreme Leader extended his arms in the Moslem attitude of prayer, lifting his hands, palms up, to heaven. *Why, oh why, Allah, have you allowed such indignities to be heaped upon your servant?*

When the Guardianship Council was assembled, the Supreme Leader's plan to sack the director of SAVAK and replace him with the IRIA commander was unanimously approved. It was also agreed that any further mention of the six American spies in the Iranian press would be composed personally by the Supreme Leader himself.

49

Aboard the *Roya*

Konarak

Amir eyed the large black man standing next to Hamid, who was looking down into the cabin at two other men and a woman—*and* two foreboding-looking rifles. Speaking Farsi, he asked Hamid, "Who are these people? Are they friends of yours?"

"They are," Hamid answered.

"Do you know a great many Americans?" Amir asked.

"What's he saying?" Cole asked Hamid in English.

"I asked him if you Americans were friends of his," Amir replied in passable English.

"You speak English," Hamid observed in the same language.

"I speak many languages," Amir said. "Sport fishermen come to Konarak from many countries, after all. But especially Canadians, some Americans, and a few Englishmen come to Konarak for the fishing. It is just good business to have some English."

"Well then. English it shall be," Hamid said. "Yes, these Americans are my friends, and we need your help."

"Is what you want from me not legal?" Amir asked.

"I am afraid our government would not approve," Hamid responded.

Amir grinned broadly, all yellow-toothed. "Then what must I do?"

"Just take us out for some fishing," Hamid answered. Amir just held his yellow grin.

"Has he brought anything to eat?" Cole asked Hamid.

Amir looked at Cole and nodded in assent. Disembarking, he went to his still-loaded moped on the dock. He brought back a large brown paper sack. "This was to be our lunch," he said to Hamid, in Farsi, as he handed the bag to Cole.

"Thank you," Cole said earnestly, and went down into the cabin, where the four Americans tore into the bag's contents. Amir then went back onto the dock to unload the rest of the moped's burden of bait and ice.

Footsteps.

Amir looked down the dock, back toward the town. "Someone is coming," he whispered loudly to Hamid in Farsi. "Army. Two of them. Tell the Americans to stay in the cabin, and to be quiet." Hamid did just that.

The two soldiers approached, one an IRIA first lieutenant. Amir greeted them in Balochi, and the two men gave him a confused look. Amir switched to Farsi. "Good morning, gentlemen, to what do we owe the presence of the Army of the Islamic Republic this morning?"

On hearing Farsi, then two soldiers relaxed. "We are looking for some American spies," the first lieutenant replied. "Three of them. Two men and a woman. They murdered five men during the night. We think they are still here in Konarak. Have you seen or heard anything unusual?"

Murdered five men? Amir thought, and remembered the two rifles. He said, "No, I have not seen anyone nor heard anything out of the ordinary."

"Well, if you do, report it to the police at once."

"I will," Amir said, and stood aside as the two soldiers continued on down the dock.

Amir returned to the task of unloading the moped. "Tell the Americans to stay out of sight and remain quiet," he told Hamid after he climbed back aboard the dhow. "The soldiers may be back." Hamid conveyed the message, though it was hardly necessary.

There was some commotion farther down the dock. Hamid and Amir saw that the IRIA first lieutenant was loudly berating the crew aboard one of the Iranian Navy patrol boats. He apparently felt that they and their compatriots in the other boats should have been underway and out searching for the Americans. The Navy sub-lieutenant was pleading his case that no one had informed the Navy that there were any American spies about. Eventually the IRIA first lieutenant threw up his hands in disgust and proceeded on down the dock. Hamid and Amir smiled as the sub-lieutenant threw an obscene gesture at their backs of the two departing IRIA men.

"I hear a bunch of boats," Cole called up, *sotto voce*, from the cabin. "The Iranian Navy out lookin' for us?"

"Apparently not," Hamid answered. "And apparently they have no intention whatever of doing so. What you hear is the first of the fishing fleet returning to port. They must have had a successful night, because they are returning early."

"And that," Amir added, "is our cover for leaving port. We are far less likely to be noticed if we are just another boat in the water." Hamid nodded in agreement, and Amir quickly started *Roya's* engine, cast off the lines securing her to the dock, and headed her out into the bay. The Americans stayed below in the cabin and out of sight, and remained below even after *Roya* had cleared the bay.

The weather was clear, and the bay waters had been dead calm, but once in the gulf, there was a slight chop. Amir registered his annoyance when John Tindal threw up on the cabin deck. Hamid wondered whether Amir was more annoyed at the mess that Tindal had made, or that Tindal's share of a perfectly good lunch had been wasted. But he didn't dare to ask.

"Where shall we go?" Amir asked.

"Head straight out," Jake called up from the cabin. "The sooner we're in international waters, the better."

"Roger that," Cole agreed. Three of the Americans, at least, were happy to leave *Roya's* meager cabin as soon as they were out of sight of the other boats. John Tindal, apparently not at all a good sailor, remained below, despite his wife's pleas. "You'll feel so much better in the fresh air," she cajoled, but Tindal refused to budge.

Just over an hour later, Amir announced that he was certain they were at least twenty kilometers offshore and in international waters. Jake got on the radiotelephone. It was 0842.

"Exodus Base, this is Exodus Alfa. Over."

"This is Base," came Clegg's raspy voice. "Where you been? You missed your 0800. Over."

"We were still in boat traffic at 0800," Jake said, stretching the truth a bit. "But we're in international waters now. Need rendezvous point for pickup, Base, over."

"Roger that, Alfa. Wait one. Out"

Then, after several minutes, "Exodus Alfa, this is Exodus Base. Over."

"This is Alfa. Over."

"Proceed to rendezvous point 24.918-869, 60.504-322. I say again, grid position 24.918-869, 60.504-322. Got that, Alfa?"

Jake entered the numbers into his radiotelephone. "Roger, Base, grid posit 24.918-869, 60.504-322. Over."

"Correct, Alfa. A Charley-Charley-Mike off of the *Mesa Verde* will be waiting. Over." [A CCM—Combat Craft, Medium—off of the Landing Platform, Dock (LPD) *USS Mesa Verde*, would be waiting at the rendezvous point.]

"Roger that, Base. One Charley-Charley-Mike at the rendezvous. Heading that way. Out."

The GPS in the radiotelephone indicated a compass heading of 142 degrees true to reach the rendezvous. Amir set *Roya* off on that heading.

Fifty-four minutes later, Cole spotted the long, low silhouette of the CCM a point off the port bow. "I think that's our ride," he announced.

There was a Navy doctor aboard the CCM waiting to tend to Jake's wounded arm. As the boat headed back toward the *Mesa Verde*, he examined the wound. "Looks good. Whoever cleaned you up did a good job," he said. "But I'll give you a shot of antibiotics just in case."

"I don't need stitches?" Jake asked.

"Nope," the doctor said, "The butterflies closed it up nicely. It should heal just fine as is."

* * * * *

Once their passengers had been transferred to the CCM, Amir turned to Hamid, and said, "Well, Mr. Alinejad, that was an interesting morning's work. What shall we do the rest of the day?"

"Well, Amir," Hamid replied, "I believe we came out here to fish, did we not?"

"We did indeed," Amir agreed with a yellow smile. "And now, Allah willing, we can lace into a nice big tuna."

50

Washington, DC, Tel Aviv, East Beach

The president made a great show of parading the rescued missionaries, along with Rep. Robert Longstreet, in front of the White House press corps in the Rose Garden. It was one of those rare late autumn days when the weather in Washington was pleasantly mild, and the sun shone brightly.

Clayton Rogers served as spokesman for the group, and thanked the country, the president, and, in particular, the brave Navy SEALs who had rescued them. He parried any questions about their treatment in Iran with the response that the missionaries would be issuing a complete written statement concerning their ordeal later. None of the SEALs were present, the president explaining that the Navy didn't want to disclose their identities and possibly jeopardize future covert missions. Some members of the press corps thought they smelled a rat, but, for a change, none spoke up. The president had been known to suspend White House press credentials when particular individuals annoyed him.

The president's approval ratings shot up in the polls, this with the general election only weeks away.

* * * * *

IRNA, the official news agency of the Islamic Republic of Iran, issued a statement that the Republic had released the six Americans being held on espionage charges to Swiss authorities on humanitarian grounds. The Swiss neither confirmed nor denied the report.

* * * * *

The president was livid. His face was almost the color of the red polo shirt he was wearing. "The Navy is going to do *what?!*"

The secretary of defense attempted to calm him. "But Mr. President, he did disobey a direct order —"

"The man made a decision in the field not to abandon an American citizen to the enemy. It was exactly what he *should* have done, and exactly what *I* would have done! Even got wounded by the enemy in the process. And the Navy wants to give him a Letter of Reprimand? Not while I'm Commander-in-Chief, Gordo! Not while I'm Commander-in-Chief!"

"Yes, Sir, but in doing so he endangered himself, his subordinate, and another civilian. And most important, in doing so, he violated a direct order. That merits a court martial! A Letter of Reprimand is peanuts compared to what the Navy could have done. They're letting him off lightly, Sir . . ."

"Letting him off lightly? That's bullshit! The man deserves a medal — not a Letter of Reprimand!"

"That's not the way the military works, Sir . . ."

"Well that's the way it damn well *will* work as long as I'm Commander-in Chief! And thanks to him, Gordo, I may just be *in* this job another four years." The president paused for effect, the way he often did. "Do you hear me? Gordo, are you listening? There will be no Letter of Reprimand, or any such thing placed in Lawlors's file—Hell, I want to give the man a medal. Him and that Chief of his—What's-his-name."

"Cole, sir. Yes, sir."

* * * * *

A call came in to Shlomo Rosenszweig over a secure line. In an unusual move, the Mossad director had ordered that a field agent call him directly when it was safe to do so. The source of the call, he knew, was in southeast Iran, but it had been relayed through several friendly and unfriendly stations to his office in Tel Aviv, the last routing coming through Damascus.

"Shalom, Director. This is Victor, calling from station Seven Zed." Station 7Z, Rosenszweig knew, was that day's code for Iran Station, and "Victor" was Yitzhak Morgenstern, a Mossad agent known to the Iranians as Hamid Alinejad. Victor was, he knew, his man in Iran who had been a guest in the Konarak hotel that had served as Colonel Farshid Salehrad's temporary quarters.

"Shalom, Victor. How goes it?"

"Very well, Sir, thank you."

"Very well indeed, Victor. Without the information you and the agents in Teheran provided, and your timely assistance just when it was needed, the Americans could never have pulled this whole thing off."

"They almost did not. I could have done more to help them had I known the woman was in the hotel to begin with, but the situation had pretty much played itself out when I came upon the scene. The SEAL lieutenant had already been wounded, and the colonel was already dead.

"Just as well, Victor. That way the Iranian police can in no way suspect you of anything other than just enjoying a vacation sport fishing."

"That is true. But I had to take a calculated risk and break cover to the Iranian boat captain."

"Who is now collecting a nice monthly stipend for his service. A small price to pay for the enormous favor the Americans now owe us. And in the process we are also free of that devil, Salehrad, eh? And SAVAK has, for now at least, fallen into disfavor with the Iranian leadership."

"Again, Director, very true."

"Well, Victor, I just wanted to add my personal 'well done' to that of your immediate superiors. Well done, Victor! Your country is indeed grateful."

"Thank you, Director, it means a great deal to me coming from you."

Now all Victor had to do was find a suitable apartment for the *zaftig* young woman who had accompanied him to Teheran from Konarak.

* * * * *

Jake opened the door to his apartment, and Moses ran out into the hall to greet him, first mewing, then purring loudly and weaving between his legs, marking him as his own the way cats do.

The door to the next apartment opened, and Julie O'Leary appeared. "Moses," she said, "I can hear you purring even with my door closed."

249

Jake looked up from the cat and saw Julie. Perhaps it was for the first time, really. He knew then, that if he didn't at least make his move, and ask her to at least consider marrying him, that he would spend the rest of his life regretting it.

"Julie," he said, "I know we hardly know each other." He took a deep breath. "And, that, since we met, we've spent more time apart than together . . ."

"C'mon, Jake Lawlor, spit it out, what is it you're trying to say?"

"Julie, what I do is dangerous, and I could be called out at a moment's notice . . ."

"And I would never ask you to do otherwise, Jake, never. Being a SEAL is who you are."

Lost for words, he went over to her, took her in his arms, and kissed her. She folded into his embrace and returned his kiss. Moses threaded his way between two pair of legs, still purring loudly, and marking both of them with his chin.

When they finally broke the kiss, Julie leaned back, looked Lt. Jake Lawlor, Jr., in the eye, and said, "I thought you'd never ask."

"I haven't, yet," he said, choking back a grin.

"But you know you will," she said, smiling.

"Damn straight," he said, and kissed her again.

About the Author

Gene Masters is a retired consulting engineer living in East Tennessee with his wife, Ruth. They have two grown daughters, and two grandchildren. He is the author of several technical treatises, including his doctoral dissertation. *Operation Exodus* is the second of three novels, coming on the heels of the highly successful *Silent Warriors: Submarine Warfare in the Pacific*. The author's most recent release is *The Laconia Incident*.

Masters received a commission in the U.S. Navy on graduation from Notre Dame, and his first tour of duty was aboard a transport in the Western Pacific. His second tour was aboard a recommissioned and updated diesel-electric submarine, the *USS Angler*. *Angler* was originally commissioned in 1943, and made seven war patrols in the Pacific before being decommissioned. Her updating to an SSK-class boat in the 1950s fitted her for operation against cold war submarine adversaries with advanced soundproofing and sonar. Masters left *Angler* and active duty after a Mediterranean tour. Later Naval Reserve assignments included the diesel-electric submarines *USS Manta* and the *USS Ling*.

After active duty, Masters pursued a career in engineering, and served in various companies until settling into a career as a consulting engineer. He retired in 2009. Readers interested in learning more about the author and his books can visit his website at: www.genemasters.net.

NOTE FROM THE AUTHOR: I'd just like to remind readers that reviews are an author's lifeblood. If you've enjoyed this book, please take the time to post a thoughtful, positive review on Amazon.com, or anywhere else you think it might be helpful. Thanks in advance for your review.

-Gene

Also by Gene Masters

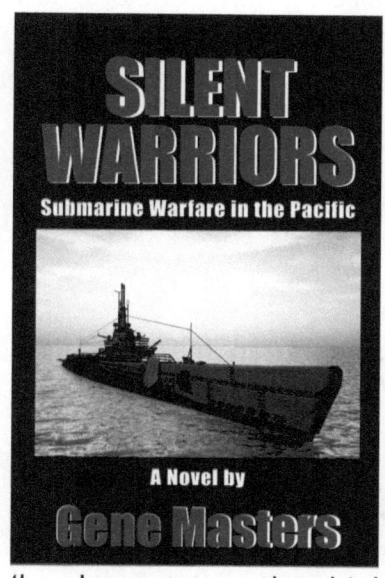

SILENT WARRIORS: SUBMARINE WARFARE IN THE PACIFIC—The year is 1941. Shortly after the United States declares war on Japan in response to Pearl Harbor, Japan's Tripartite Treaty allies, Germany and Italy, declare war on America. The United States finds itself in a two-theater war. President Franklin Roosevelt sets as America's first priority the defeat of Nazi Germany, electing to wage a more-or-less holding war in the Pacific. In the beginning, the only force opposing the Japanese onslaught in the Pacific is the U.S. Submarine Service.

Jake Lawlor begins the war as executive officer aboard *USS S-49*, an aged *S*-class submarine, with orders to conduct unrestricted warfare against the enemy in the Pacific. When a freak, mid-sea grounding causes the loss of *S-49*, Jake assumes command of *USS Orca*, a new *Gato*-class submarine under construction in Groton, CT. As Jake prepares a new boat and a freshly assembled crew for war, the conflict in the Pacific is going badly for the Allies.

This is the story of Captain Lawlor's eleven war patrols, including an ongoing conflict with Imperial Japanese Navy Captain Hiriake Ito of the destroyer *Atsukaze.* The crew of the *Orca* is made up of grizzled veterans and wet-behind-the-ears youngsters, all working together for a single purpose: to bring an implacable enemy to its knees. Along the way, friendships are forged, and love affairs and marriages are created—and destroyed.

Pour yourself a glass of your favorite libation, grab a comfortable chair, and enjoy a tale that's sure to hold your interest in *Silent Warriors: Submarine Warfare in the Pacific* by Gene Masters, now available in paperback and Kindle from Amazon.com, and as an audiobook from Audible.com.

Kudos for *Silent Warriors: Submarine Warfare in the Pacific*

* * * * *

Well-Researched Novel about submarine warfare in the Pacific during World War II

"Silent Warriors is primarily concerned with following the fictional World War II exploits of Jake Lawlor, a 1933 graduate of the U.S. Naval Academy. When we first meet Jake, he is the Executive Officer (XO) aboard S-49, a twenty-something year old boat on her first war patrol in the very early days of America's war in the Pacific. The sub has just run into a coral reef, the victim of an old, outdated chart. Jake soon finds out that, much to his relief, that the Navy, in the process of gearing up to fight a war, is prepared to be a bit more forgiving to the officers of a sub that suffers such a fate than it would have been in peacetime. He soon finds himself promoted to Lt. Commander and given command of the Orca, Through most of the rest of the book we follow Orca through a wide variety of assignments on her war patrols. We sweat out many tense moments, and can celebrate some well-deserved high points.

Unlike many books of this particular genre, which tend to concentrate on the attacks and subsequent efforts to avoid destruction, this book gives us some insight into the lives of the men who operate her, as well as a few glimpses into the other side of things, with many scenes from the Japanese perspective. Throughout it all, the author gives us short descriptions of the actual events of the war in the Pacific that were taking places during the time of the fictional exploits recounted in the novel. This technique gives the reader a great sense of historical context for the main story.

If you are a fan of World War II submarine warfare, or even bit of a history buff, this is a good book. The author takes pains to dig a bit into the lives of many of his main characters, with the deepest dive, naturally, into Jake's life. It is well-researched, both from the historical context the author gives the fictional events and in terms of what it was like to serve in one of these denizens of the deep that played a vital role in the war effort in both the Pacific and the Atlantic."

—Old Coot in Norcross

* * * * *

"Ah-oo-gah, ah-oo-gah, dive, dive!"

"Silent warriors is an ambitious historical war novel that focuses on the US submarine service from 1941 to 1945 while at the same time providing glimpses of the broad arc of US operations in the Pacific theater. Gene Masters draws on his expertise as a veteran submariner aboard diesel powered submarines to bring to life what it was like to be aboard a Gato class boat, at that time the finest submarine ever built. The author does a masterful job in evoking the cramped life aboard a submarine: "space was at a premium, filled with equipment and material of every sort, and living spaces appeared to be an afterthought for the boats designers... Sleeping racks... were wedged between torpedoes... water was in limited supply... when submerged the air became rank... After two days at sea, bodies were ripe..." Additional tidbits evoke the inherent danger of diesel submarines: leaks caused by external hydraulic pressure, highly flammable hydrogen fumes from the batteries, and mechanical malfunctions at depth which could be fatal. The book chronicles the technological improvements made to submarines during the course of the war: active sonar and radar to name only a few. During Orca's travels throughout the Pacific the boat requires repairs from battle damage or resupply in ports where the crew enjoys liberty and the reader follows along visiting exotic places such as Brisbane and Port Moresby.

The plot centers on the main character, Jake Lawlor, graduate of the US Naval Academy 1933, a cool and intrepid naval officer who takes command of the Gato class submarine, Orca. Once this newly commissioned submarine completes its sea trials, Lawlor takes command and his submarine completes eleven diverse missions, for the most part associated with the major battles in the Pacific: Midway, Manila, Guam, Tarawa, Iwo Jima, Okinawa, Yap, Guam, the Solomon Islands etc. That is not to say that the Lawlor submarine participates directly in MacArthur's island hopping invasions of Japanese occupied islands. The reader learns very quickly that submarine warfare operates as a support arm of the Navy, operating on the periphery of the bloody, troop-mounted frontal assaults on Japanese held beaches and islands. Rather, submarines operate by stealth, lying in wait for enemy transports and convoys, then sneaking up and firing torpedoes which were not always accurate (the Mark-14 even had defective trigger mechanisms). In response to these ambushes, Japanese destroyers responded with depth charges which often proved deadly to the fragile, US underwater craft. The Orca completed many of these search and destroy missions with great success as well as many unconventional missions such as mining Manila Bay and landing a search and rescue team on the Philippine island of Mindoro. The reader is also treated to love affairs, marriages, and the life of a Navy family when the submariner is at sea.

The novel's dramatic tension derives from all the unknowns the Orca faces as she goes about fulfilling her missions: the major question being whether the submarine will survive its many deadly encounters with Japanese anti-submarine vessels. The answer is only given to those who read the novel.

Silent Warriors is a fascinating, informative and exciting novel and I recommend it to all readers interested in military fiction and/or history or who just want to experience the life of a WWII submariner."

— Lloyd R. Free

THE LACONIA INCIDENT—It's mid-September 1942. A German U-boat, U-156, sinks a converted British ocean liner, HMT Laconia, with just two torpedoes. The captain of the sub is horrified to discover that the troop transport he has just sunk was carrying 1,800 Italian POWs, along with British and Polish passengers and crew.

Why the sub captain chooses to launch an operation to rescue his surviving Italian allies is perfectly understandable. But why he also chooses to rescue the British and Polish survivors is truly a mystery. How and why he pursues the rescue while convincing the German U-boat command and Adolph Hitler to go along with it is an even more illogical conundrum.

This then is the basis for "The Laconia Incident," a story with complex ramifications that just go to show that truth, indeed, is stranger than fiction. Read this amazing account and learn the facts behind the apparent "fiction." The answers will intrigue and amaze you!

Kudos for *The Laconia Incident*

* * * * *

Humanity shines through during the perils of WWII!

"The Laconia Incident is a well written true story that centers around the sinking of a British transport ship off the West Coast of Africa by a Nazi submarine during WWII. The transport was carrying a large number of Italian prisoners of war along with British citizens, including military personnel from Britain and Poland.

What stands out in this story is the triumph of the human spirit in the face of the horrors of war. All of the characters portrayed are caught up in doing their duty as citizens and soldiers on each side of the conflict, but as they are thrust into the realities of war their ability to look at their enemies with mercy overcomes the inclination to view their enemies as objects for destruction.

During this dramatization of true events we meet characters, who for the most part, become heroes in their own right as they struggle to do their duty while remaining humane. We meet British sailors and civilians, Polish and Italian soldiers, German U-Boat Captains and the German High Command, including Hitler, Vichy French Officers, and American Army aviators.

For those interested in the telling of events that are a hidden part of the great cataclysm of WWII this book will be an informative and entertaining read."

— Yiassou